The Red Earth

HARPERVIA

An Imprint of HarperCollins*Publishers*

The Red Earth

A Novel

Morgana Kretzmann

Translated from the Portuguese
by Daniel Hahn

 For information, address HarperCollins Publishers, 195 Broadway, New York, NY 10007. In Europe, HarperCollins Publishers, Macken House, 39/40 Mayor Street Upper, Dublin 1, D01 C9W8, Ireland.

HarperCollins books may be purchased for educational, business, or sales promotional use. For information, please email the Special Markets Department at SPsales@harpercollins.com.

hc.com

Originally published as *Água turva* in Brazil in 2024 by Companhia das Letras.

First HarperVia hardcover published 2026

Designed by Yvonne Chan
Plant illustration © Florilegius/Getty Images

Library of Congress Cataloging-in-Publication Data has been applied for.

ISBN 978-0-06-343798-2

Printed in the United States of America

26 27 28 29 30 LBC 5 4 3 2 1

Contents

The Romanos

Gringa Romano

Enrico Romano + Galliana

Caco Romano

Thales Romano

The Sarampiãos

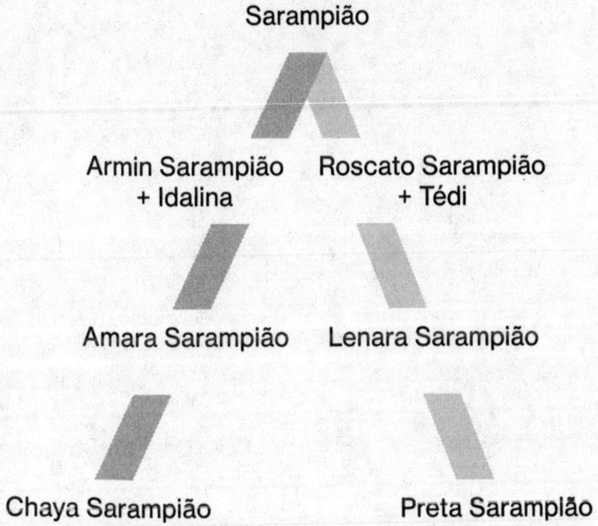

The Red Earth

Land

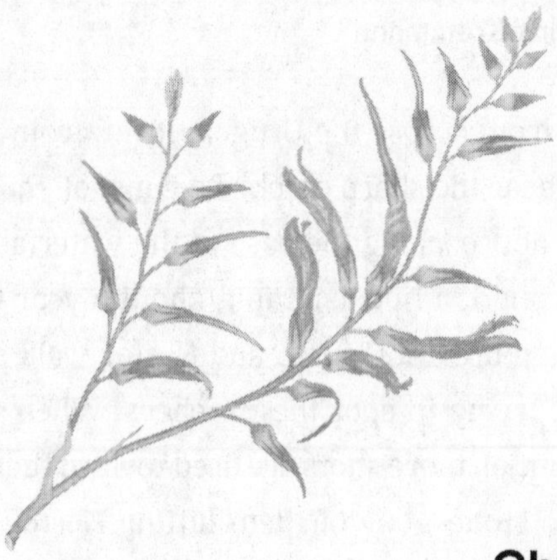

Chaya

Bastards — that's the last time they come hunting round here. . . ." Chaya Sarampião floors the grimy white pickup, its doors emblazoned with the shield of the "Forest Rangers — SEMA." Gripping the wheel tightly, she deftly weaves around the holes and stones of the muddy earth road.

"Today's the day we get 'em," she promises Ângelo Alves, the new head of the Turvo park team, who sits shotgun, and the two other rangers, Cláudio and Nestor, in the back. They hear gunshots followed by an animal's shriek coming from somewhere near the Sarampião waterfall, one of the most densely forested areas in the park. Chaya yanks the handbrake, making the tires skid. The truck stops crosswise on the road. She kills the engine. The four rangers climb out, guns drawn. Chaya gestures to Cláudio and Nestor to bring up the rear. The recent budget cuts mean that the two men have had to spring for their own bulletproof vests. Used ones, from across the Uruguai River, from Moconá, in Argentina. They hear the sharp crack of a gunshot and move further into the bush, approaching the base of the waterfall. The water roars. On the ground, a midsize tapir, about a year old, lies bleeding, still drawing breath. Cláudio and Nestor walk slowly, looking around them, trying to spot the poachers. When the two men are near the animal, more shots are fired toward them. The bullets ricochet off the stones, one of them hitting Nestor's vest. He falls. Chaya and Ângelo respond to the gunfire in kind, while Cláudio helps his companion, dragging him behind a cedar trunk. They hear shouts in Portuñol, the blended language so common in that border region:

"No shooting! Por favor! No shoot!"

Ângelo stops firing. Chaya keeps going.

"Stop, soldier!" Ângelo orders her. "That's enough."

She does stop, but her gun stays up, held out in front of her.

"Show yourselves — hands in the air."

A wide-eyed adolescent appears with arms raised.

"Where are the others?" Chaya walks over to him, still not lowering her gun. The boy begs her — "Ay, help me!" — and points to the red bromelia bush behind him. Ângelo signals to Cláudio and Nestor. The two rangers advance cautiously until they see a man stretched out on the ground. He's moaning. There's blood on his neck, spilling over the dry leaves and the red mud. Next to him, a .38 revolver.

"Poacher down, captain," Cláudio calls out.

"Any sign of others?"

"Nothing, sir."

The adolescent, still in Chaya's sights, starts to cry. A crying that is tormented by the shock that overwhelms him.

"Help me!" He chokes on his own despair.

Cláudio and Nestor pick up the wounded man and place him beside the now dead animal. The man's entire body starts to shudder.

"He's going into shock," says Cláudio.

Within seconds, his breathing stops. The boy drops, catatonic, to his knees, and in the meekest of prayers, he babbles:

"Papá? Papá? Ay, wake up! Hombre, wake up!"

Chaya looks at the son, at the father, then back at the son. She sees herself in that despair, in the brutality of that scene.

"Ugh, fucking hell. *Shit!* Oh shit, I don't believe it!" She lowers her gun.

Without hesitating, Ângelo raises his own gun to point it at the kneeling boy. Cláudio takes hold of the man's wrist in search of vitals.

"He's gone."

"Fetch the tarp and the shovels from the truck. We'll roll his body up, and then bury the tapir," says Ângelo.

Cláudio and Nestor obey and disappear into the forest. The boy is still on his knees. His face is soaked, a mixture of sweat, tears, and snot run down his lips and chin. He looks at Chaya and asks:

"Why? Es un animal, was only animal . . . just for food . . ."

Chaya doesn't answer.

The boy picks a rock up from the ground. He faces Chaya again and says: "You!"

She draws her gun. The boy doesn't drop the rock. The seconds pass, until Chaya allows herself to be struck by the impact of that look, of that scene, refusing to normalize the barbarity of which she's a part, the price of the word unspoken, of the action already committed. She holsters her gun before crouching down, then sitting, her head between her legs. Ângelo, who still has the adolescent in his sights, is watching Chaya, appraising the little body of his colleague with the fine, coppery skin, who's not yet thirty, wearing a bulletproof vest that's two sizes too big. He does admire her, professional that she is — her uniform always impeccable, her black hair long and smooth, tied into a bun, insisting, despite the precariousness of the job, that she's serious about the exhausting day-to-day of being a ranger in that remote, forgotten part of the interior of Brazil. A strong woman who shouldn't allow herself to be affected by the fragility of that moment.

Chaya closes her eyes. She drags one hand across the mud — a mud that's dark burgundy, typical of the Turvo park — then picks up a handful, brings it to her nose, and inhales. A flock of caciques flies overhead, singing. She looks up.

"Arrê . . ." she mutters to herself, as her grandfather Armin comes to her mind, with his voice and the old accent of somebody raised amid the toil and the bush, right here in this region. "Arrê, Sarampião." She gets up, still holding the damp earth. "We're letting the kid go."

Ângelo is wordless, as if unable to understand what Chaya has just said. But then he tries to formulate a sentence: "I think . . . we're . . ."

"We are letting the kid go!"

Ângelo huffs, takes off his cap, exposing his gray hair. With the back of his hand he wipes the sweat that's trickling down his face.

"Look, do I need to remind you *I'm* the fucking boss in this park?"

She shrugs. She's heard this so many times before, from so many bosses who've passed through this place, she's lost count.

She positions herself between her colleague's gun and the adolescent. Ângelo's face flushes.

"Hey, cabocla!" he shouts. "Now your insubordination's going too far!"

Chaya clenches her jaw, feels the hostility emanating from Ângelo's voice.

"You can do what you think you need to do later, captain, whatever disciplinary action, against this . . . *cabocla*," she says, taking her gun from its holster. "But I'm freeing this kid and nobody's going to stop me, not you — especially with less than six months under your belt." She turns to the boy: "Run. Tell your mom or some other relative they've got to come pick up your dad's body at the Dourado IML. You get me? You get me?"

The boy stands up, still holding the rock, he takes two steps backward, wiping his eyes and nose with the hem of his T-shirt. His expression changes. He looks at the officer. Ângelo fires into the air. Chaya turns toward her colleague. The two officers look at one another. The boy runs toward the bush and disappears into the trees.

"You can put your gun away, captain," she says and throws down the earth she was still holding. "I come from this place, I know what needs doing here and how it's gotta be done."

Unconnected thoughts swirl around Ângelo's mind. He focuses on the man and beast lying dead, side by side, on the blood of one mixing with the blood of the other, both being absorbed by the earth. The dry eye of the animal and that of the man, their bodies already being covered by the litterfall moved by the strong morning wind.

Olga

The phones don't stop ringing on the secretary's desk in the offices of the chief of staff and the press team, where Olga Befreien is sitting.

From inside his office, with the doors closed, Deputy Heichma yells:

"Is everyone fast asleep out there?"

Olga gets up sharply, her leg knocking into the desk. She curses. She goes over to reception and finds Ana Paula deeply engrossed in her phone. She walks over to the little office where Senna, the chief of staff, is calmly smoking, turned toward the window and the sun behind the two blue buildings of Rio Grande do Sul's administrative center. Olga knocks on the wall. Senna turns to look at her. She points to the ringing telephone.

"Well, why don't you answer it, then?" Senna asks, and he takes a drag on his cigarette.

Olga raises her eyebrows, thick and black like her hair, walks over to his desk, and her eyes still fixed on him, lifts the phone from its cradle: "Deputy Heichma's office, good afternoon?" She hears what the person on the other end of the line has to say, gives a very definite "Absolutely, we'll get that done," and hangs up. Senna asks who it was. She doesn't answer. He repeats the question. Olga goes out toward the deputy's office. She knocks on the door, and without waiting for permission, turns the handle and goes in.

"Excuse me, Deputy Heichma, Dr. Elpídio called," she says, leaning against the doorpost. "He says he's tried to talk to Senna several times but he never answered. He said to tell you, senhor, you've got till December." The deputy gestures for her to come inside and shut the door.

Heichma gives the impression of a man who is gradually melting. Sweat is trickling down his forehead and the flabby cheeks that stick out from his face, just as his belly sticks out, his shirt buttons almost popping loose. The smell in the room is sour milk.

"Got your little headlights on, eh?" He laughs and reaches over to tweak one of her nipples, prominent under the white blouse and the unpadded bra.

She swats his hand and — as vulnerable as a confused, ashamed child, not sure whether she has done something wrong — crosses her arms, hiding her chest.

In the underground garage beneath the Legislative Assembly, Olga takes the car key out of her pocket and unlocks the car. She tosses her purse, her phone, and a pile of folders into the back. Bits of paper, photographs, and spreadsheets scatter across the seat. She gets in and starts the engine. Once she's on Rua Riachuelo, she reaches for the phone she'd thrown in the back and tries to slot it into the holder attached to the dash. It falls onto her lap. Olga notices that her arms are trembling more than they've done in other similar situations — which have become more and more common this past year. She stretches her neck right, then left. It cracks. With the car in motion, she unhooks the phone again, opens her contacts, and makes a call.

"Hey, Mom. Is Dad there? I need to talk to him. . . . Yeah, all fine. . . . I just told you, it's all fine! . . . Hey, Dad. How's the beach? . . . Did you go fishing? . . . At Rosa or Ibiraquera? . . . So, here's the thing, I'm going to Dourado. . . . Right! That's why I'm going. Nearly thirty years old already, diploma on the wall, and all for this . . . Good! So if you don't mind, I'm gonna need you to ask those two buddies of yours to go to the hydroelectric meeting in the morning. . . . Ugh, man, it's such a crappy old town. . . . Oh yeah? Well, if it was really that great, you guys never would have moved to Santa Catarina, now, would you? . . . Hey, I've got to jump off, Heichma's on the other line. Love you."

She hangs up and the sound of the other call gradually increases in volume. She takes a pack of cigarettes from the glove compartment. Her hands still trembling, she extracts one and lights it. She opens the window and puffs out. Then she turns on the radio, full volume. The phone keeps ringing.

Night falls on the BR-386 and traffic on the road is light, unusually so for a Thursday. Olga is pushing 140 km/h when she realizes she's almost out of gas. She stops at a gas station on the roadside somewhere close to Montenegro.

"Fill it up, please," she says before heading inside and asking for a coffee. The bitter, stale taste slips down her throat, and she spits into the cup. "*Just pay for your food and let's get going*," she hears some guy next to her saying. "*We'll refuel at Santa Rosa.*" A shiver runs down her spine. It's nobody she knows, but the timbre of the voice and the accent are just like the deputy's. She feels a burning in her nipple, the sense that she's being pinched again. The same shame. She goes over to the drinks cooler, gets a water and a Red Bull.

In the car, she downs half the bottle of water. She picks up one of the files from the back seat. There's no way she'll be able to study all those documents, she thinks, not before the meeting tomorrow morning. She turns on the interior light and reads:

GRAN RONCADOR HYDROELECTRIC POWER-STATION

THE BIGGEST BINATIONAL HYDROELECTRIC

COMPLEX IN THE SOUTH OF THE COUNTRY

OUR BELOVED NATION OF BRAZIL

Next to that line, the huge logo of the federal government.

"Why are those Dourado settlers so against this?" she wonders aloud. She tosses the folder back. Lights a cigarette. She opens the can of energy drink, takes a gulp. She starts up the car.

Caboclo Arrê

Ten p.m. and Chaya is in one of the bedrooms at the Turvo park rangers' lodge. The brick building, painted beige and with wooden windows, is used by the officers to spend the night when they're on duty in this conservation area. She sits down on the lower bunk, runs her hands over her itching legs. Then she runs her fingers over her eyebrows several times. She shuts her eyes, pictures the violet sky that's typical for October in the northwest of Rio Grande do Sul. Nothing helps. She can't get the face of that Argentine teenager out of her head, nor the blood spurting from his father's neck. And what if she had stopped firing, what if she'd held back? she thinks. Her arms itch. She rubs herself, scratches. Then she interlaces her fingers and counts to ten out loud. Twenty. Thirty. It doesn't work. The man's lifeless body, soiled with earth and blood, still weighs heavy.

She gets up slowly and moves over to the desk, where she finds a candle and a match. She walks out barefoot, first on the cold floor and then on the grass, taking advantage of the bright full moon on that Thursday night, until she comes to the queen palm. She looks up at the thick branches, then kneels and rests her hands on the ground. Tilting her head forward, she speaks:

Arrê, old Sarampião
Arrê, Arrê
Oh caboclo, Arrê
Protect the Turvo
Altar place of everything
Faith-man
In the forest
Cure the land
Cure the water
Cure it Sarampião
Arrê, Arrê.

She lights the candle and sits there for a time just watching the flame, accompanied by the sound of the night: the park's crickets, frogs, and owls.

In the Fog, Warnings

Close to midnight, Olga drives through the gateway into Dourado. The low nighttime mist makes the place a ghost town. On Avenida das Viuvinhas, the main road, the only lights on are streetlamps. In the square, it's possible to make out, dimmed by the fog, the statue of Sarampião and of a jaguar beside him, and a fountain designed to look like a section of the Yucumã Falls.

She turns onto Rua Cauré and stops outside the Jaguar Hotel, which is shut. Even the famous animal-shaped lamp is off. She switches to her high beams and flashes three times. The main gate opens. A short man, with long arms, wavy red hair, freckled skin, around thirty, appears.

"Olga Befreien — it's been ages!"

She gets out of the car, smiling, and hugs him.

"Thales Romano! You look different. Taller." Olga laughs and ruffles his hair.

"And you look the same!" He puts his hand on her waist.

Seven o'clock on Friday morning. Olga is at the hotel's German breakfast buffet. A mug in her right hand and a slice of homemade bread with pumpkin compote in her left. She takes a bite, chews slowly. Then she picks up the stack of papers she ought to have read by now. Thales comes out of the kitchen and sits down opposite her.

"Good morning," he says, rubbing his hands to dispel the morning cold still lingering on that early spring day.

"It's not *that* good, I didn't sleep a wink," she says.

"Eh? So what were you up to all night?"

"Haha, very funny."

Olga pretends to be focusing on the documents. Thales doesn't take his eyes off her.

"So, about today — you needn't worry. But just remember, the people who're going to be there don't want to hear big words, OK? Let me have a look at what you have," and he takes the document from her hand. He goes on: "Drop all this stuff about those downstream businesses, IAP, RPA. You know what it's like — people think difficult talk is you trying to pull the wool over their eyes. Really all you need to say is you're here on behalf of the deputy."

"I'm not only here on behalf of Heichma. I'm here on behalf of the whole NEP bloc," she says.

Thales chooses not to reply and looks straight at her. His thoughts are wandering. His father, Enrico Romano, was one of the people who'd founded the National Environmental Party in the state, but he ended up leaving politics because he thought it would be bad for business. The current mayor of Dourado is also from the NEP — an outdated acronym that despite its centrist-progressive origins supported the candidacy for president of a man from the far right, with no experience or political expertise, famous for fronting up a sensationalist cop show on TV for almost two decades. There was widespread hysteria when he got elected, followed by a conservative lurch by politicians and parties from an assortment of ideological positions, who opportunistically rallied to support him, all across the country. It was no different with Deputy Heichma, no different with this party. The whole platform once championed by the NEP got distorted, distanced from the original program, and the concessions toward the environmental dismantling in Brazil have come to be tolerated on a pretext of more jobs and greater progress. One of this administration's priorities is the building of the "Gran Roncador" hydroelectric power station in the small district of Centro Novo, twenty kilometers from Dourado. The project has been on hold for ten years, not only because a chunk of the Turvo State Park, along with the homesteads of many local farmers, will end up underwater, but mainly because of the threat it poses to both the jaguar's habitat and to the widest waterfall in the world, the Yucumã. It was the falls that gave the Gran Roncador hydroelectric project its name — in Guaraní, Yucumã means "the great snorer."

Thales touches Olga's fingers. "I think you should stay till Sunday. Go to a few folks' houses, visit with some community leaders, farmers. You should talk to locals, not outsiders who don't get this place."

Her phone rings — Deputy Heichma appears on the screen. She answers.

"*Morning! You still on the road?*"

"Why?"

Thales waves a hand, gets up and leaves.

Heichma goes on:

"*Easy now, girl! It's just I woke up early and I thought to myself, ah, my little Olguinha has already forgotten all about her Deputy.*"

Olga picks up the coffee cup, notices her hand trembling. She tries to answer, but her voice catches in her throat.

"*I want you coming back to Porto Alegre today with good news*," he states firmly. "*I trust your powers of persuasion. I know you'll be able to convince your fellow countrymen to accept the dam. I'm expecting you for dinner.*"

Olga hangs up without saying goodbye. She glances at the papers on the table and contemplates hurling them across the room, along with her phone. She tries to focus on the future, on her reasons for staying in Heichma's office, and thinks once again about her freedom, about the professional and financial stability she's going to have when she's finally employed as a reporter at TVE/RS — Rio Grande do Sul's state TV station — having been through the public service exams two years prior. A security that only a career in state television could guarantee. Something she could never achieve anywhere else — this is something she believes utterly. But according to the rules of the political game, today, Heichma is the only person who can determine whether she gets the job or not, since the president of the state network, besides being from the same party, owes the deputy favors, and he's the man with the pull to allow Olga's name to appear in the Official Gazette. So while she does ask herself *How long will I be able to hold out?*, her objective is quite clear.

You're not giving up now.

She bangs on the table, gathers up her things, and goes back to her room.

A Snubnosed .38 and Boots

Two hours later, Olga arrives, alone, at the community center at the Lutheran church. She is wearing dark glasses, black knee-high boots, and a cherry-red jacket with gold buttons, fitted to her body. She's holding the folders crammed full of papers. When the people filling the hall — most of them rural workers, in jackets, woolen cardigans, hats, caps, jeans, and ankle boots well-worn from hard use — turn toward her, with no sign of friendliness or acceptance, she concludes that she has chosen her outfit well. The idea was to distract from what she isn't going to say, seeing as she doesn't know *what* to say, and draw attention to something else, *anything*, even her flamboyant clothing, just the sort of clothes you'd expect to find on those stuck-up people from the capital, people who are no longer welcome here.

Besides the community themselves, there are officers from the state military police and soldiers sent in by the federal government. The atmosphere is tense. Representatives from local schools, from business, as well as municipal environmental and community councillors, are sitting in a circle. The soldiers are standing behind them.

Olga manages to spot her father's friends, Aldo and Irineu. They're standing by a wooden table with some others who she thinks work in the mayor's office — as had been agreed with the deputy — and also a man from the association of northeastern municipalities, toward whom she cannot hide her expression of contempt. She walks over, drops the folders on the table, and greets each of them with a handshake.

They are joined by the local secretary of infrastructure, Maurício Ricci, who went to school with Olga and is the son of the former mayor, Claudenir. She can't help laughing when she notices the almost cartoonish contrast between the man's huge biceps and the exaggerated thinness of his legs, emphasized by his tight jeans. He arrives with Júlio, environmental engineer, representing the Gran Roncador power-station consortium. Everybody exchanges greetings. Maurício makes a goading comment, adopting his usual position as a mafia bigshot who knows he's the boss of this town:

"Hmm, I don't seem to see Heichma. How come he's not here?"

"It's already past nine," says Olga. "Let's start."

Maurício tries to disguise the fact that he's been ignored and takes the lead, talking loudly so that everybody hears him.

"Everyone — it's time. Settle down now."

There's a bit of hubbub. Olga and the men who are to run the meeting sit facing the community. Maurício introduces the guests, then he steps closer to the people and says:

"So, everyone here knows me, and you all know my dad, former

Mayor Ricci. I was born and raised in this town. A town with potential to grow, to develop, to have industries, and universities, and all the jobs they'd bring you all too. Dourado already has the first conservation area established in the state, our beloved Turvo State Park. We've already got Yucumã, the largest longitudinal waterfall in the world. But what's missing? What's missing is structure, and investment, and money to make tourism here be more like they've got up in Foz do Iguaçu, for starters. Everything they've got there is thanks to the Itaipu hydroelectric power station, and now we're being given the same opportunity: a binational project that will bring countless benefits to Dourado and the entire region."

"Now look here, kid, I respect your dad, I do, I voted for him — but you got a long way to go before you can speak for him or for us," says Orlando, a well-known local dairy farmer. "There's no comparison at all. We're talking about nineteen different municipalities that are gonna be hit by a dam that nobody here knows hardly anything about. If Gran Roncador really did get built, it'd only produce the tiniest amount of energy. That's in the studies we commissioned ourselves. The project's budgeted at more than five billion U.S. dollars. Wouldn't all of us be better off if the government just invested that money directly into local businesses, schools, and infrastructure, here and across the whole region?"

Maurício has no answer to this. His face flushes. He looks to Júlio and Olga for help. Olga doesn't move from her chair, just pulls her phone from her pocket and pretends to be reading something important. Júlio gets up.

"Good morning — my name's Júlio and I'm responsible for the environmental impact study you've all received. I'd like to begin by saying what a pleasure it is to be here to answer your questions, to try to assuage any doubts about the building of the Gran Roncador dam, and to tell you a bit about the techniques of sustainable innovation that will be used to avoid harming the environment and the community. Because our main concerns are socioenvironmental."

The sound of heavy footsteps. Júlio stops talking, and all eyes turn toward Chaya, who appears in the hall. She's in uniform: pants and jacket in camo print, a white shirt, and a cap. Mud cakes the sides of her boots' soles and their leather tops. Her gun is holstered at her waist.

"Good morning! Good morning to my people. Sorry I'm late. Júlio . . . It is Júlio, right?" Chaya faces up to Júlio. "Ah, we just love that word round here, don't we? '*Socioenvironmental.*' Don't we all love it, folks? Well, so how's about you start off by explaining the interview that came out in today's paper, then, where you say that, in order to make up for the area of the Turvo park that's gonna disappear forever, thanks to this venture of yours that's *oh so very 'sustainable'* . . ." Chaya says, pulling the newspaper out of her back pocket and starting to read: "'the federal government will be purchasing agricultural lands and donating them as compensation for the portion of the park affected. It's all very simple after that, merely a matter of chucking around some seeds and all the vegetation, the trees, it'll all just grow on its own. We'll have a technical team of soldiers and civil professionals — handpicked by the president of the republic himself — who will be in charge of that.'"

The community watches, annoyed; the soldiers nervously exchange glances.

"And as for the disappearance of the Yucumã, the threats to the jaguars and the other wild animals? Nothing to say about them?" Chaya goes on. "I'm sure we'd all love to hear what you got to say.

Go on, then, Júlio, let's hear what you have to say about the Yucumã and about . . . your little *seedlings*," she says, handing the newspaper over to one of the community leaders.

The engineer's voice comes out in a squeak:

"They've taken those words out of context. It's fake news. I'd never speak for the Brazilian army, or for our president."

Chaya gestures for the community to stand up. Everyone walks toward the exit. Only Chaya herself stays put, arms crossed, legs spread, facing down the police officers and the soldiers. When the last resident leaves, Chaya registers each of the authorities there, one by one, until she comes to Olga. The two of them take a good long look at each other. A look that refuses to give way.

"Welcome back, Olga," Chaya says, needling.

Olga doesn't answer. She's paralyzed at the sight of the woman before her. Chaya turns on her heel and leaves, disappearing into the glare of the hot sun blazing outside.

Preta

Midday. After leaving the public hearing, Chaya returns to the park and hurries into the office. She picks up the radio and calls Dóris, the officer from Dourado civil police who's in charge of the IML.

"Thanks for coming to the park to fetch the body."

"*The freezers here are full up, Chaya,*" Dóris tells her. "*He'll be getting a pauper's burial.*"

"What about the thirty days? Like it says in the law?"

"*Man, you asked me to do this totally illegal thing, and now you want me to abide by the legal time limits?*"

"Hey, I'm sorry, pal, I really am — but it's complicated, you know that. I'm gonna have to get across the river, over to the Argentine side. . . . Can you hang on a little longer?"

"*You're really going over there to talk to her?*"

"I've got to."

"Well, you shouldn't. But I know you, no one's gonna shift that idea once you got it in your head. Just get it done today, OK? Before Friday's out. You've created a major pain in the ass for us both."

Chaya steps into a small boat that had been hidden among the branches and the fallen trees at the old Pari port, a shingle beach that's been closed to the general public since 1954, when the former forest reserve was upgraded to the Turvo State Park. It's blowing a gale. The Uruguai is raging, its water crashes against the hull of the small wooden craft, soaking part of Chaya's body. She makes the crossing to Argentina.

When she reaches the other side, she moors the boat to a nearby tree, tucks her revolver in the back of her belt, hidden under the jacket of her uniform, and climbs a track up the steep bank, then through the dense trees, till she reaches a huge rocky outcrop in the middle of the forest, a site of a scenic beauty that even someone like Chaya who's been here her whole life can't help but register. On the ground, carved into one of the rocks planted in the ground, is written: *Red Foot Territory*. Another fifteen minutes of walking and she starts to hear the chorus of barking dogs and children's laughter. A man with hair that falls to his shoulders, a mustache, and a faded blue fisherman's hat appears before her. He's holding an old Bersa rifle. He looks Chaya up and down. She brings her hands up to her chest:

"I'm here to talk to your leader. Tell her I come in peace."

There are fifteen houses, some of them wooden, others built out of old containers with improvised zinc porches, all packed close together. In the center, one grimy wooden house is painted in the green of the Brazilian flag; in front of that, a bonfire with a large square pot held by iron bars. A woman somewhere in her forties, tall and strongly built with her brown hair tied in a long braid, is bent over the fire. She is wearing shorts, a tight T-shirt, and rubber flip-flops. Preta stirs the food, an offal rice, with a wooden spoon. The smell of kidney, gizzards, liver, tripe, and heart all fried together overpowers Chaya. Without stopping what she's doing, and without looking up, Preta speaks:

"Been a while."

Chaya and Preta are sitting on a fallen tree trunk by the side of the green hut. Each woman has a plate laden with food. They chew unhurriedly. The children and adults are scattered about in front of the other houses. They too are eating. A five-year-old girl spits out a piece of kidney and tosses it away. Two dogs scramble to retrieve the offal and fight over it. Preta gets up, goes over to the child, and gives her a smack on the mouth. The girl's dish flies from her hands. The dogs run over and gobble up the leftovers.

"Little devil! Now you go hungry."

Everybody looks at Preta, then they lower their eyes, saying nothing. The child gulps back her tears. Preta returns to her spot.

"It's not easy keeping order, teaching the value of things."

"This is what you always wanted, Preta, isn't it? Your grandma would be glad to see you like this, keeping charge of everything here," says Chaya. "I'm really sorry about her, by the way, about Tédi."

"It's like it's just happened."

"It's been years since we've talked." Chaya takes another spoonful.

"Would have stayed like that too, if I'd had my way."

There's an unease between the two women. Each inspects the other's face, turning over conflicting feelings and memories, a geography of occurrences separated by the Uruguai River.

"Well . . . you do know why I'm here, don't you?"

"I'm not going over there to identify the body." Preta spits on the ground.

"To *fetch* the . . ."

"Or to fetch it." Preta gets up. "Forget it."

Preta doesn't trust the Brazilian police, nor the Argentine police for that matter. Here, in the border zone, where the rules are made and broken by her and her alone, nobody challenges her freedom or the freedom of her group. Two factions — armed and dangerous — have tried to invade Argentine territory here, one of them Paraguayan and the other Brazilian. It is the Red Foot, under Preta's leadership, who've managed to protect this area and to prevent a war from starting, some years back now. In exchange, the people with the real power there, the ones in charge in that border zone, don't mess with her or with her business. Leaving could be dangerous for her.

"He was your man, Preta. Wasn't he?"

"I've had others."

"Nobody's going to give you any trouble on that side, I can assure you of that. . . ." Chaya puts the empty plate down on the tree trunk and gets to her feet.

"Stooge. You know where you can stick your *assurances*. You come to me talking this crap now? After everything that's . . ." Preta moves away, not taking her eyes off Chaya. Deep down, neither of them wants to venture into that kind of conversation. But they know they're only putting it off: They'll have to get the past resolved sometime. Not enough years have gone by to close up the wounds. "And it's not like you're even a real cop," she concludes.

Chaya moves toward Preta, their faces almost touching. "I'm as much a cop as those cops who want to lock you up."

Preta presses her forehead against Chaya's and says quietly:

"I know what you would do. I know whose granddaughter you are."

"Wash that mouth out before *ever* mentioning my grandfather again." Chaya pushes the leader of the Red Foot, but she — bigger and stronger — grabs the officer by the arms, immobilizing her. Chaya tries to pull free, and Preta throws her aside. She staggers and almost falls. She threatens to launch herself back onto Preta again, but doesn't move. She thinks about her own grandfather Armin. Memories rise up of when she was six. Blood. Tears. Then she once again remembers that other man in shock, dying in the park yesterday. The blood spurting from his neck. The boy crying. She's suddenly dizzy. As if she might fall. Her hands search for something to lean on. Preta holds out an arm. Soon Chaya focuses again, and the two women stand there, facing one another. Their guards drop. Downcast, they share the same look in their eyes — a look that is desolate.

"That kid who was in the park, I know he's nothing to do with you, I guess he's just another one of those stray animals who wanders aimlessly around the border. But it's his damn *father* that's there in the IML, rotting." Chaya takes a deep breath.

"His name's León," Preta replies.

The boy appears at the door to the green-painted house, walks down the wooden steps and over to Preta, who takes one of his hands. León and Chaya look at one another.

"He told me," says Preta.

"Told you what?"

"You shot his father."

Chaya feels her back aflame as if a blowtorch were running down her body. She starts sweating again. She takes a step toward Preta.

"So he'll be getting a pauper's burial, then."

"And you're the one to blame for that!"

"He shot first."

"That's your justification?"

"You know the park has rules, Preta! Laws! Fucking hell, cuz," says Chaya.

"*Cuz*?," says Preta, mocking. "Wow, you really have got some nerve." She pushes León aside. "We might look like a pack of *animals*, like you say. But our flesh is worth more than the flesh of a wild pig. Take care, Chaya, there's always a price to pay."

"Arrê! I'm trying to preserve this park, like Sarampião did."

"Arrê! You still think you're Lady Justice, and using our great-grandfather's name to justify your mistakes."

Chaya feels those words like a blow. She shouldn't have come, she should have listened to her friend Dóris. If only she wasn't so impulsive. So eager to change things. But no past can ever be changed.

Preta goes on:

"You and all those rangers should be thanking me. A kilo of each paca, tapir, peccary, dorado, catfish, in pesos, cash — ultimately that's what supports all these people here, so they don't need to get mixed up in running guns or drugs. And that's my law."

"Ugh, give me a break, Preta. And the booze?"

"Oh, go to hell! That's just dodging a bit of duty, anyone could be mixed up in that, even your beloved old Romano."

"You really believe in this rotten little world of yours!" Chaya loses it now, shouting. "In this blessed, immaculate territory that you and your grandmother invented. You present yourself as everybody's savior, you think you're queen of the marginalized. But you're a fraud. You got a past too, Preta, and you and me are the only people here who know what it is."

Preta digs her nails into her own forearm until the skin breaks and bleeds.

"Get out of here before I . . ." She stamps on the ground, raising a cloud of red dust.

"I just want to get the matter of the body resolved. That's why I've come."

"You really think that trick's going to work? Bringing the dead man here, his throat ripped apart, it's not going to intimidate us. We're not gonna stop hunting."

"And I'm not going to stop shooting at whoever goes in there."

"Course you won't. You've turned into a Romano. Changed your name on your birth certificate yet? Sarampião would be ashamed. You aren't — you never were a real red-foot caboclo like me, like us. Get out of here. Scram!"

Chaya feels her heart pounding, her face burning. She pulls the gun from the back of her belt and points it at her cousin. Three women and a man appear, all of them armed, but she is not intimidated.

"It's not just a river separating us, Chaya, it's reality too," says Preta. "Look around. My reality and yours will never meet."

"Why don't you tell them to shoot?" Chaya doesn't lower her guard.

Preta puts both hands on the back of her own neck. Her bones are aching. Her eyes show the torment of someone both burdened by the past and overwhelmed by their ability to foresee the future. Her voice hoarse, she says:

"Your destiny isn't on this side of the Yucumã."

Chaya recognizes that look, that voice. She frowns. She puts away her gun and walks into the forest, toward the river. Preta, León, and the rest, all motionless, watch her. Before Chaya disappears from view, Preta calls after her:

"We are the Red Foot, we go out each day ready to kill or to die."

"In that way, we're alike."

Preta spits on the ground. She hears the Uruguai River in the distance, and the flies and mosquitos buzzing around her. She returns to the pot where there's still some offal rice left. She scrapes the wooden spoon along the bottom, the burnt rice, and throws it to the dogs. The animals approach slowly, fearful. They eat without quarreling, eyes fixed on the chief.

1957

When It All Began

Death, the Coward, and the Wise Man

Sitting on a tree stump, round the back of a wooden house painted in an earthy hue, on the bank of the rivulet beside the Turvo park, Sarampião is looking at nothing. Armin comes out of the house carrying two mugs of water. He hands him one and settles down beside him.

"It'll be good for you to take on the ranger's job in the park, Dad," says Armin. "But wouldn't it be better to wait a few days? It hasn't even been a month since Mom died."

"I can't stand being inside. I go into the bedroom and she's not lying there. I can't even remember what your mom was before that illness. Everything here stinks of death."

"It was a lot of years. But Mom was happy here too. We were happy here."

"So why don't you bring your family?"

"I'm only just done plowing, Dad, I'm just starting to plant. How am I supposed to leave the land now?"

"You're right. Let's let your brother and his family come."

"Oh, Roscato won't take care of it, he'd only end up selling the place."

"Arrê! Have some faith, child. He's changed."

"If you say so."

The two men sit in silence.

"Living inside the park, that's always been a dream of mine," says Sarampião.

"It's brave of you, Dad. Place is full of jaguars, every kind of creature."

"I know this forest like the back of my hand. And its animals too. Turned out lucky for me the last ranger here was begging to leave."

"I'd have done the same if I found myself face-to-face with a rat snake in the kitchen. The man spent hours on top of that table," Armin laughs.

"Guy didn't understand a thing."

"He was just a bit slow, Dad."

"An ignorant fool, and a coward. Wisdom is the privilege of a very few."

"That's how I know you'll make the best ranger this park has ever seen."

Sarampião and Mad Mouth

Sarampião runs down the newly opened trail through the dense forest of the Turvo park. He's in worn old ankle boots, his pants folded up over his shins, an unbuttoned shirt. His coppery skin and his smooth hair, which flows down over the nape of his neck, gleam as the sun's rays catch them. On his back, fastened with a thick leather strap, he's carrying a 36-gauge, loaded with birdshot.

"About time to bring the hunt for old Mad Mouth to an end once and for all. Those filthy white folk . . ." Sarampião mutters to himself as he leaps over branches and bushes.

He hears a growl. He stops running. He tilts his body forward, spins around. There's another growl behind him. He turns.

"It's been a while, old girl." He looks into the cat's yellowish eyes. They stand motionless, her with canines bared, him with his lips closed. Both breathless.

The moment of tension between them is broken by a long shrill whistle. Sarampião and Mad Mouth break eye contact. The jaguar runs. Sarampião follows her. The animal disappears into the trees. The man leaps over a fallen trunk, struggles through mires, dodges spiderwebs, passes through patches of prickly vegetation. Very out of breath now, sweating and scratched, he hears the animal again, and then a gunshot, and another. His eyes mist over. His body loses balance and he topples to one side.

When he comes to, he's lying on the ground, on damp leaves. He feels hot breath close to his face. With some difficulty he turns his neck to one side. He sees the jaguar. He smiles. He places his hand on his belly. The hot blood is flowing.

"Arrê . . ."

Drunk men, their guns raised, laugh as they pose for a photo. One of them is holding the muzzle of the jaguar, which is strung upside down, its legs tied and hanging from the top rafter of the large shed round the back of Gringa Romano's grocery store. From its slit throat, the blood drains into an aluminum bowl. Caco Romano, with red hair and pink sunburned skin covered in freckles, proudly displays the animal's huge tongue and gives the order:

"Go on, snap that picture quick."

"Just waiting for your brother to sort himself out," one of the men says.

Enrico Romano, though still a kid, is the spitting image of his older brother. He stands rooted to the ground, paralyzed, his eyes fixed on the blood slowly filling the bowl. Another man moves away from the group and comes back with a toolbox and a pair of pliers, which he hands to Caco. He stretches open the animal's mouth, and though it's not easy, he pulls out the upper right canine.

"Now let's take this fuckin photo."

The two huge wooden doors open, making their rusty hinges creak. Armin Sarampião appears wielding a machete.

"Where's my dad?"

Caco tosses the pliers aside and puts the tooth away in his pocket.

"What you talkin about?"

"Dad was round my place early today and went out to look for Mad Mouth."

"Seems I beat him to it, then." Caco points at the jaguar. He and his friends laugh.

Gringa Romano, a tall woman of around fifty, with thick arms and legs, gray hair tied up on top of her head, her skin covered in freckles, comes in. Everyone goes quiet. She walks over to Enrico and the jaguar, looks at the animal with a bullet hole in its chest and a straight, deep knife cut across its throat. She grabs the boy's arm, pushes him forward, toward the door.

"Get out of here."

He doesn't contradict her, and leaves.

Gringa kneels down in front of Mad Mouth. She leans over and murmurs something that no one else can make out. Caco watches it all without blinking. Still on her knees, the woman looks straight at her older son, then gets up. His friends take a few steps back, frightened. She turns to Armin.

"I'm going to round up the men from the town and we'll go into the park. And we won't come out again till we find Sarampião. I promise you that."

Four weeks later, in the small Lutheran church of Turvo town, the community is on its feet. They are talking quietly in small groups.

Seated on the front bench are Armin Sarampião, his wife, Idalina, and their six-year-old daughter, Amara, her greenish eyes damp from weeping. On the adjacent bench are Roscato Sarampião, a tall man, broad-shouldered with big hands, and his wife, Tédi, blond, thin, with striking features, holding her daughter Lenara, aged twelve. With her smooth black hair and a square face that bears the family sadness, Lenara is the one who most resembles her grandfather Sarampião. Enrico, Caco, and Gringa Romano are all standing together, at the back. The minister comes in through the main door, and walks slowly till he stops in front of the altar.

"Good afternoon!" The minister picks up the Bible from the table. "Let's all take our seats. We're all gathered here together today not to celebrate but to entreat. It has already been a month since our ranger and, to many, well-respected healer, here in our community, left us. Let us pray for his . . ."

"No! My granddad's right there!" Amara shouts, interrupting the priest and pointing toward the Turvo park.

Armin picks the child up and carries her to the back of the church. Idalina follows him.

Roscato shoots daggers at his brother, then turns his eyes back to the minister and speaks in such a way that everyone can hear:

"I apologize for my brother and his family and their lack of manners, minister. Wherever he is, I'm sure my dad's very grateful to see everyone here."

Armin looks at Roscato sadly. He puts Amara down, and the girl clings to his legs. Idalina, in turn, runs her hands over her daughter's shoulder.

'You're wrong, brother. This whole gathering's all wrong," Armin says.

He, Amara, and Idalina head for the exit. Caco calls out to him:

"You're going to leave this ceremony that we've orga — "

He's silenced by a pinch from his mother.

"Shut your mouth!" Gringa says.

Armin looks right at Caco.

"And you, you're gonna get what's comin to you. Just wait . . ."

"OK, man, take it easy now," Gringa interrupts him.

"Everyone here knows Sarampião was in the Turvo to save Mad Mouth from these pieces of shit. You got dirty hands, I know it," Armin yells, sticking his index finger in Caco's face.

"Shitty little caboclo . . ." Caco tries to launch himself at Armin, but he's pushed aside by his mother, who is indisputably stronger.

"Get out of here!" Gringa says.

Caco is still enraged, but he obeys her. Enrico follows him. Gringa, with visible restraint, speaks to Armin, Idalina, and Amara:

"Apologies for my older boy. When I was widowed, I ended up pampering him and he got spoiled. Armin, my friend, I understand your mourning."

"I'm not in mourning!"

"Please," begs the minister, "let's all calm down now."

"Sarampião is a Red Foot," says Armin, "he was raised in this place, and he's out there somewhere. And he'll find some way of coming back."

Armin, Idalina, and Amara are walking through the forest. Lenara is following on behind. They walk until they hear the sound of the Yucumã Falls. They walk round the crag beside the Uruguai riverbank to stand in front of the water.

Armin kneels down, rests his head on one of the rocks and weeps.

"Arrê, Sarampião — where are you at, father?"

His wife and daughter watch the scene and cry together.

Lenara approaches, and stands there, saying nothing. Amara watches her for a time. She takes her cousin's hand. The two girls turn toward the forest, they rest their eyes on the Turvo park and smile.

Gringa is sitting in an armchair by the window of the living room of her house in the center of the town of Turvo, behind her grocery store. Caco walks in, wary. Gringa does not look at her son.

"You called for me?" he asks.

Gringa doesn't reply. Caco goes on:

"Mom, you'll have to forgive me but there's no way I'm apologizing to that gourd-skin . . ."

Gringa gets up from the armchair, takes two steps, raises her eyes, and with her open hand gives her son a slap in the face, making a deep and hollow sound. Caco stumbles at the impact of the blow and falls to the floor.

"It was your twenty-eight gauge, wretched boy. . . ." She kicks him in his ribs.

"Stop it, Mom!" Caco shouts. "It wasn't! It wasn't mine!"

Gringa is irritated and heads for the bedroom, fetches a leather belt, and beats her son's legs until the metal buckle comes loose and strikes Caco's upper lip. The blood is spreading over the stone floor and his shirt.

"Whose was it, then?" Gringa asks, her voice hoarse.

Caco says nothing. He spits up some bloody drool. Then he takes a deep breath and speaks:

"Ask Roscato!"

Enrico appears on the porch and asks:

"Why Roscato?"

Destiny Traced in Blood

Winter. Amara has been afflicted for the last three days with a high fever. Armin harnesses his two oxen, Zebruno and Branco, to the cart. He calls out to Idalina.

"I'm off to Gringa's store for some medicine. Enough waiting."

"Sarampião would know what herbs to use."

"Well, turns out my dad's not back, so for now we'll just have to figure things out as best we can." Armin kisses his wife's cheek.

He gets up onto the cart and takes the dirt road that runs parallel to the park.

"Off you go now, come on now, come on . . ." he calls to the animals.

Two kilometers later, on the second bend, he hears a whistle. He pulls on the reins, the oxen stop. Another whistle. His stomach tenses. He gets down from the cart and walks into the scrubland toward the sound.

"Dad?"

All he hears is the sound of the forest.

"Sarampião?" he asks again.

He takes another few steps. He hears a jaguar growl. His eyes widen, and he runs back.

Back on the road, he finds the cart and oxen no longer there. He sees the two animals tearing off back toward his home. Armin looks once more at the forest. The doubt he's been carrying with him for months resurfaces. He still believes his father has a kind of divine credit on this land: a little while longer.

He takes a deep breath and runs after the animals.

"Here, here now, Zebruno! Here, Branco!"

Twenty minutes later, Armin arrives home panting. Before he has even recovered his breath, Idalina comes out to meet him.

"He's back," she says, "he's back."

"Who, woman?"

"Sarampião."

"Arrê."

Armin throws himself into the house. He looks in every room. He enters Amara's bedroom, and freezes. His daughter, in bed, has a plaster on her chest made of green leaves and mud, and another, bluish, covering her forehead. He approaches and notices a cup on the bedside table with a dark, strong-smelling liquid.

"Well, child?"

"Hi, Daddy."

"Where is he?"

"Who?"

"Your grandpa."

"I dunno, Daddy."

"Amara . . ."

"I just woke up and this was here."

Armin sits down beside his daughter. He takes the plaster off her forehead and places his hand on it. It's cool to the touch.

The earth-colored house that used to be Sarampião's is starting to suffer from the lack of upkeep. A few planks from the back wall are coming loose. On the kitchen floor, beside the wood stove, there's a hole revealing the dark damp earth. Roscato appears, reeling. The stench of strong liquor mingles with the room's scent of burnt firewood. Tédi watches him, worried. Lenara has been running a fever for days, aching, and with a loud wheezing in her lung. The look on her mother's face betrays the pain of somebody who has lost one child to illness already.

"Roscato, for the love of God, go into town, talk to Gringa, see if you can get some medicine. And some bones with marrow to make this kid a soup."

"With what money, Tédi?"

"You can make some charcoal and deliver it to her later."

"Oh, so that what happened last time can happen again?"

"Do *something*. Our daughter is sick."

"That pest is always sick."

"If Lenara ends up underground with her brother, it'll be your fault."

Roscato smacks his wife's face. She collapses. He grabs her hair and drags her to the bedroom where their daughter is lying.

"All this is your fault," Roscato yells. "It's that bad blood of yours. Our children were born broken because they came from inside *you*." He releases his wife and staggers out of the house.

Tédi gets up, still lightheaded, lies down beside her daughter, on the bed with the straw mattress, and hugs her, trying to get her warm.

Roscato makes his way along the dirt road that leads to the grocery store in town. His steps are heavier than usual. With his straw hat, and stooping, his face is hidden. He enters the store, walks right up to the counter. He puts his hands down on the countertop and drums his fingers, making an irritating sound with his nails. Enrico comes out of a door behind the counter. He gets up onto a little stool so he's at the same height as the cash register. He watches Roscato's fingers still tapping on the wooden surface and asks:

"What d'you want?"

"Call your mother."

"Say what you want, Roscato."

"It's '*senhor* Roscato,' to you. You show me respect, a crummy little brat like you. . . . Now go in there, get Gringa, I don't deal with kids. Go, 'fore I wallop you," he shouts, hitting the counter hard.

Caco appears from behind a beige curtain hanging across the door to the storeroom.

"What's with the commotion?"

He and Roscato face up to one another. Caco pulls his brother off the stool.

"Go in and weigh the coffee and the sugar," he tells him.

"One day I'm gonna cut your hands off," says Enrico, "filthy drunk." The boy looks at Roscato with loathing and enters the storeroom Caco had emerged from.

"One more year and he's really gonna do it," Caco laughs.

"That brother of yours has no manners."

"Whoa, man, what's making you so nervous?"

"Where is she?"

"My mom's gone into town."

"Lenara's sick."

Caco says nothing. Roscato has used this story about his sick daughter to swindle food, drink, and money at least a dozen times before.

"I need medicine, food, and a little money. I got charcoal cooling. I'll deliver it in just a few days," Roscato continues.

Caco picks up an old notebook with a dark cover and leafs through.

"There's things of yours in here from two years back."

"I've paid a good chunk of it. Gringa must've forgot to cross it off."

"You're sayin my mom's trying to pull a fast one on you?"

Roscato clenches his fists.

"I know things that could bring you a whole world of trouble, you goodfernothing . . ." says Roscato threateningly.

"Huh — pretty bold! If I told half of what *I* know, the folks in this place would lynch you, and I'd just stand and watch."

Roscato snorts. He spits on the floor. Then he taps his fingers on the countertop again. And stops. He lets his arms drop to his sides and makes one final attempt.

"Man, I just wanna buy some medicine and food."

"Buy? You've come here to beg for charity. But actual work? Nah, you don't want any of that, do you?"

Roscato takes off his hat. He runs his hand through his sweaty, greasy hair.

"My mom's already said, you can clean the pigsties over at the farm . . ." Caco can't complete his sentence before he starts laughing.

"You think you're such a big shot," snarls Roscato, "but you're just a dumb fucking Romano who can't do a thing right."

Caco's laughter grows.

"I'm the son of Sarampião," Roscato continues. "Whose son are you, eh?"

"You're a useless caboclo, that much is for sure. An idler, a layabout. Even the house your dad gave you to live in you ain't taken proper care of. Sarampião was ashamed of you when he was alive. Get out of here. And take a bath — see if you can shift that stink and that filth from off your back," says Caco.

Curious passersby wander into the store to find out what's going on. Roscato puts his hat back on his head. He leaves. He walks around behind the larger building that houses the store. Round the back, he opens the door to a shed and goes in. Two minutes later, he comes out again, holding a machete.

Caco is chatting to a group of three men who came in shortly before Roscato left. An elderly woman crosses the threshold, walks over to the counter, and hands him a piece of brown paper. Caco calls Enrico out to serve her. The boy climbs back up onto the stool and spots the notebook with Roscato's name still sitting on the counter. Roscato bursts into the store. The two brothers barely have time to see the icy look in the man's eyes. Eyes that are lifeless, trained upon their destiny: Caco's neck.

Caco's blood is flowing onto the countertop, the notebook, and Enrico's face. Caco puts one hand, and then the other, over the cut.

He tries to ask for help from the younger boy, who's standing paralyzed, but he can't do it. He falls at his brother's feet.

Tédi's eye is dark and swollen. She prepares a basin with soap and water to wash her child. She goes into the small bedroom and is surprised to find Lenara with a plaster of green leaves and mud on her chest, and another, this one blue, on her forehead.

"Who put those on you?" she asks, but gets no answer.

She runs through the house.

"Sarampião? Sarampião?" She returns to her daughter, and asks again: "Who was it?"

"What?" Lenara's voice is weak.

"Was it you or was it him? Tell me."

"I'm tired."

Tédi hears clapping from outside. She cracks a smile. When she steps out onto the porch she finds her brother-in-law, but before she is able to speak, Armin asks:

"Is he here?"

"Sarampião?"

Armin finds this strange. He looks around the outside of the house, then in it.

"Roscato. They're after him."

Karma Doesn't Forget My Name

Some months later, Gringa Romano is in the driver's seat of an old pickup; beside her sits Armin Sarampião, and behind them, Tédi and Lenara. The road is irregularly paved, and the deep dips make their bodies sway from side to side. They enter a neighborhood set back from the center of Dourado and arrive at a beaten dirt road with an open sewer, both sides of the road crammed with dozens of houses, made of zinc sheets, wooden boards, leftovers of wood laminate. They stop in front of a small brick house, its walls unplastered. The sun is hot, the day stifling. Lenara looks all around. Her angry eyes come to rest on these new surroundings.

The residents of the street come out in front of the shacks. The children run up to the truck and stare at its four passengers curiously.

Gringa and Armin get out first, they open the back and start to take out the luggage. Lenara and Tédi pick up their bags from the ground. The teenager drops everything and puts her arms around her Uncle Armin.

"Please, can I go back with you?" she begs him.

"Leave him, child." Tédi pulls Lenara away.

Gringa Romano takes an envelope out of her back pants pocket and hands it over to Tédi.

"Here's your bit of what was left from selling Sarampião's house. There was that big sum owed to the grocery store and all the rest, but I let the oldest bills slide. This'll be enough for you and her to live a few months without having to worry. Just don't forget what we agreed, Tédi, OK?" Neither Gringa's face nor her voice hides the fury she is feeling. And Tédi, in turn, does not hide her contempt.

"You needn't worry. I'm not goin' back to that shitty town."

Gringa looks right at Tédi without blinking, then returns to the truck.

"Better this way, Tédi," says Armin. He takes a piece of paper out of his pocket and passes it to her.

"The address of the house I told you about. Go talk to the woman who owns it. It's decent pay."

Tédi does not take the piece of paper. Armin insists. She lets it fall to the ground. Armin shrugs and walks back to the truck. Lenara runs toward her uncle and, before he has slammed the door shut, she grabs his hand.

"When can I visit Amara, uncle? When can we go back?"

Armin says nothing. He feels sorry for his niece, who will have to bear the burden of her father's karma forever.

"And what about Sarampião? He's gonna find me . . ."

Tédi interrupts her daughter:

"Quiet, kid. Stop talking such rubbish. Your grandpa's dead. Now get over here. Let those folks get on with their lives."

Armin kisses the girl's forehead and shuts the truck's door. He and Gringa leave. Lenara starts to cry.

"Hold back those tears, girl," Tédi says. "Come on, woman, be strong, have some dignity. That's the one thing they can never take from us."

"I don't want to stay here."

"We're not staying," says Tédi. "We're goin after that goodfer-nothing father of yours."

Gringa and Armin arrive back at Turvo town. Gringa turns into a road flanked by cornfields.

"Stop here," Armin tells her.

"What are you saying, man — I'll drop you at home."

"I said stop!" Armin grabs the door handle.

She brakes. Armin gets out of the truck and slams the door.

"So we're all square now?"

Gringa takes another envelope from the glove box and hands it to Armin.

"Your part of the house," she says.

"I don't want anything to do with . . ."

"This was Sarampião's. Do what you like with it." Gringa tosses the money out the window, turns the pickup around, and leaves.

A feeling of melancholy washes over Gringa Romana. She knows this is not the end. Karma is not done prowling around these two families yet.

Water

The Cabocla and the Outsider

Saturday, ten a.m. A curiously hot day in Dourado. Olga wakes up sweaty, under three heavy blankets. She throws everything on the floor and sits up, naked, on the bed. She lowers her feet to the tiled floor, then walks over to the bathroom, washes her face, and brushes her teeth. She opens the window onto the street and the warm air rushes into the bedroom. Picking up her cell phone, she sees five missed calls and two voicemails from the deputy. There's also a text from her dad. She replies:

"*Morning, dad! Yeah, it was all good. Coming back to Porto Alegre tomorrow. I'm at Thales's hotel.*"

She immediately regrets sending it. She marks the message to delete it, but two replies, one and then another, arrive before she can:

"*Haven't you learned anything, Olga?*"

"*Honestly this is impossible.*"

Her phone, its battery drained, goes black. Olga walks over to her suitcase, crouches down to take out her charger, stands back up, and feels dizzy. The two bottles of Argentinian wine she drank with Thales the night before throb into the front of her head. She leaves her device charging and goes over to the shower.

She slips on a light dress, daubs sunscreen and foundation onto her face, spritzes some perfume. She takes her half-charged phone, her purse, and leaves.

The hot sun burns. Olga gets into the car, switches on the AC. From Avenida das Viuvinhas, she turns left, onto a paved road, then a dirt track. She passes a green sign that says "Barra Bonita," with an arrow pointing toward the right.

She stops outside a white colonial-style house, gets out of the car, walks across the lawn, and claps her hands three times.

"Anyone home?"

A little man with sparse gray hair, wrinkled skin, and sunspots comes out to the yard.

"Good morning!" he calls out to the stranger standing on his lawn.

"Good morning! Senhor Benedito? Is that you, senhor?" asks Olga.

"No! You're some way off. Benedito lives a ways down the walk. I'm Josué."

Olga takes the leather notebook from out of her purse. She looks at the notes scrawled the night before. She and Thales, who by that point were drunk, made a list of all the community leaders she ought to talk to — well, more than talking, listen to what they had to say about the hydroelectric project and the real reasons for their opposition.

"Sorry about that. I'm Olga Befreien, I'm a journalist . . ."

Josué cuts her off.

"The daughter of the Befreien who had the hardware store in town?"

"That's the one," she says, with a smile.

"The girl who did that shameless thing to the statue of Sarampião and our square?"

Olga freezes.

"You thought we wouldn't remember? Get your stuff and go. You don't belong here," Josué says.

Olga returns to her car. Flashes of memory appear: the mist, the wine on the ground and the stained clothes, the broken bottles, laughter and more laughter. Olga brings her hands to her face, rubs her eyes. The memories continue: a scream and the fire. Her phone rings. It's the deputy. She tosses it onto the floor of the car.

She speeds down a dirt road that bisects a huge soy plantation. Thoughts whirl about her head while she focuses on the bends and the loose stones. Skidding, she loses control and plunges into the field. She steps hard on the brake. The engine dies. She tries to start the car back up. Nothing. She tries again. Nothing. She has no one she can call for help. There's no way she's ringing Thales now, he said he'd be having lunch with his father and with Chaya. She looks around her, trying to spot some house, or any living soul who might be passing. It's already almost noon. The temperature has broken thirty-eight degrees Celsius, which is unusual for Rio Grande do Sul this time of year. She opens the windows. A white pickup appears in the distance. Olga gets out of the car and runs back to the side of the road. She waves her arms. The truck slows. It stops. Olga frowns when she realizes it's Chaya. She's in jeans and a white V-neck T-shirt, wearing her long, smooth black hair loose.

"They're saying it's gonna storm today."

Olga says nothing. Chaya goes on:

"Best be on your way as soon as you can. The wind has a habit of exposing even the filth you thought was really well hidden."

The two women continue to stare each other down. Before leaving, Chaya smiles and says:

"Give it a shove. Try to jump-start it."

Chaya leaves Olga under a cloud of red earth that finally settles around her long after the truck has passed.

Around two in the afternoon, dirty and sweating, Olga comes out of an auto repair shop. She's smoking a cigarette, her purse hanging from her arm. She walks along the paved road beside the Turvo square, toward Avenida das Viuvinhas. She intends to get back to the hotel right away, take a shower, and wait for the repaired car to be delivered there. She glances sidelong at the statues of Sarampião and the jaguar, which are integrated into a fountain that is an imitation of the Yucumã Falls, in the middle of the square. She looks around her, but sees nobody on the streets. She walks over to the statue.

"Sarampião, I, I was an idi . . . so you know I didn't mean . . ." She hesitates. "Ugh, no, Olga — please. *No.* You never liked this hideous statue, and now you're talking to it?" She tosses her cigarette away, puts her purse down on the ground, removes her shoes, and submerges her feet to cool down, then her legs, and finally she ends up climbing under the falling water. The pressure beats down on her scalp, on her shoulders, on her back, and she smiles for the first time since leaving Josué's. And now she thinks about the significance of this town, where she was born, the only place she was ever really free. She recalls her childhood, her adolescence, and then the pain of all the constant judgment, the mistakes that cannot be undone. Town. Weight. Emptiness. Solitude. Sadness. The weight of all this still hangs in the air. Olga shuts her eyes.

She hears a voice:

"Arrê, Sarampião."

A hand grabs her neck and hurls her out of the fountain. On the grass now, she wipes her wet eyes — it's Chaya again. Olga wonders how that small body, seven inches shorter than her, with those thin arms, could have yanked her out with such strength.

She looks at Chaya in her uniform and with a gun holstered at her waist. She starts to laugh.

"Man, this town, this statue, Sarampião, the whole thing's always just been one big joke to you," snaps Chaya.

Olga keeps laughing as she puts on her socks and shoes, picks up her purse.

"You know I could arrest you for that," Chaya goes on.

Olga looks straight at her, while she takes hold of her wet hair and wrings it out, then does the same with the hem of her shirt.

"You don't own the place, Chaya."

"And you never should've come back, Olga." Chaya takes two threatening steps toward Olga and stops.

"Nobody who doesn't worship Sarampião, who doesn't kneel before this ridiculous statue to your great-grandpa, is welcome here, right?" Olga turns to leave.

Chaya launches herself at her and, from behind, grabs her right arm, twisting it furiously. Olga screams. Chaya screams louder:

"Say that again. Say it again, I dare you."

She realizes how much strength she's using, that she might

break the woman, and lets go. Olga scrambles away, cradling her aching arm.

"Have you lost your mind? Asshole . . ."

"Fine, Olga, no more fighting. Just leave once and for all."

"Fighting? You're the one who started it all. Does Thales know you openly assault people on the streets now?"

"Leave my brother out of it. Man, you brought so much unhappiness to this place years ago, and you've only come back now with more."

"What are you talking about?" Olga asks.

"The power plant and that asshole deputy you work for."

Olga shoots Chaya a look full of contempt. She pulls out a cigarette and lights it, inhaling once, twice.

"Nobody in Dourado wants that dam. And that boss of yours . . ."

Olga interrupts:

"Oh, really — nobody?" she says, mocking. "You don't know the people round here all that well, then. Apparently not even those closest to you."

"And you do? You really think people are going to forgive you? To *support* you?"

Olga can't hide her discomfort. She knows Chaya is right. Stupid to continue this conversation. She dodges her and walks slowly along the avenue. Chaya calls after her:

"Be a woman. Have a shred of dignity. You're not seventeen any more. Leave this place and take that stupid hydro dam with you."

Capa Preta

Enrico Romano, now seventy-three — white hair, tall and solidly built, muscular even at this advanced age — sits in his office at the back of the hotel. He opens and shuts drawers, folders, moves pieces of paper around. Thales knocks at the door, then barges in without waiting for his father's permission.

"Why the long face?" Thales gathers up some pieces of paper that have fallen to the floor. "Is it Heichma again? More bottles of wine?"

"Keep your nose out of my dealings with him. Here, gimme that." He snatches the papers from his son's hand. "Make yourself useful and go down to the cellar, check how many bottles of that Capa Preta we've still got."

"Please, Dad. If Chaya hears about this, you know what's going to happen."

"Your sister's no fool. She knows plenty of Porto Alegre politicians buy their wine from me."

"Buy?"

"Shut the fuck up, kid, you hear?" Enrico snaps and kicks a chair away.

Thales is surprised to find his father so on edge. All his life he has known his father to be a methodical, cool man, even in the heat of endless quarrels. Enrico has always prioritized his business above all else and manages it with a steady hand, without anybody in the family, or any employee, ever discerning any emotion from him. Thales speculates it's his father's age; he's got to slow down, take a break before he makes himself sick. He walks over to the door, but Enrico calls him back.

"Why's that girl still here?"

"Who?" Thales doesn't catch his eye.

"Heichma called me this morning and asked about her. How many new problems do you intend to create for me?"

"He's the one who sent her."

"That woman is one of those . . . you know the type. That whole business is a mess. Her and Heichma, up to their tricks over there. . . . You say I shouldn't be lying to Chaya, but I can't help notice *your* memory's been real selective lately. . . ."

Thales still says nothing.

"You're not a teenager anymore, and I'm not about to march down to some police station to clean up your mess and hide all your fuckups," Enrico warns.

Thales gets the message. Chaya wouldn't forgive him, but she wouldn't forgive Enrico if she knew the truth either. He knows how hard it was for his father to smooth over the past for the good of the family, in the hope of preserving companionship and love between the adopted siblings. Yet he hasn't wanted this from his father for a long time. He no longer wants the dirt to be constantly swept under the rug.

"I don't see why you're angry with me," he says. "We both got a lot to lose if this conversation continues this way. So let's just calm down, Dad, OK?"

"Have you forgotten who you're talking to? Man, if you'd talked to your grandmother Gringa like that you'd have gotten a beating, and a good one. Maybe that's what you needed."

"Fine, that's enough now. Olga's just here to talk to the community, about the wonders, the great benefits of this hydroelectric thing. Isn't that what the deputy wants? You should be pleased."

Thales walks out, and Enrico follows him. They hurry down the corridor that leads to the front entrance of the hotel, passing a pair of employees who greet them to no response. Enrico takes his son's arm and mutters in his ear:

"Crazy little shit — you want to fuck up my livelihood? Our lives?"

Thales looks at Enrico with infinite sadness. He admires his father's strength and intelligence. He respects his history, the way he kept the family business afloat after the death of his brother, Caco, and the sickness of his mother, Gringa, despite being so young at the time; the way he knew how to make money, implementing everything he had learned from the family matriarch; how he became such a powerful man on that stretch of the border. Thales knows he will never be the son Enrico wants. He's always comparing himself to Chaya, ever since she came into their lives, when they were both children; and his father's always comparing him to his late Uncle Caco. He never received an affectionate word, a compliment like those his father gave Caco or Chaya.

“Sorry, Dad. I spoke without thinking. You’re right. I’ll go put aside those bottles of Capa Preta for the deputy. Do you need any more wine?”

Enrico runs his hand over his son’s head then returns to his room, shutting the door behind him. He takes his phone from his pants pocket and makes a call.

“We can’t leave it till tonight. Send it over now, whatever you can.”

War

At four p.m. that same Saturday, Preta walks alone across the rocky outcrop surrounded by scrubland between her village and the Uruguai River. She stops beside the rock carved with the words *Red Foot Territory*. She's holding a shotgun pointed ahead of her. Two women and three men, all likewise armed, join her, the women positioning themselves at her side, the men behind. From the rear, ten more appear, the older members of the group; they have white hair, tattooed arms, and skin bleached by the sun. With them come the adolescents, lugging dozens of crates of wine. Another two women appear to one side, emerging from the forest. They're carrying a huge, grimy Styrofoam cooler, containing ice and pieces of tapir and peccary meat. From the same side two men emerge with another cooler containing fish like dourado and spotted sorubim, still intact. León comes up alongside Preta.

"I told you to hang back with the others," she says, pointing at the group of adolescents.

"I'm a cazador, I'm one of the hunting men!" An annoyed-looking León shows her the knife he'd been keeping hidden.

Preta slings the gun over her shoulder. She gives the boy's face a slap and takes his knife away.

"Little piece of shit, that's what you are. You're gonna end up like your dad," she says, waiting for some sort of reaction that doesn't come. "Everything round here is moved by wine, meat, or blood. Right now, your place is on the wine. Otherwise, you'll end up going straight to the blood."

León looks right at Preta, then, barging through anyone in his way, he joins the adolescents. He takes a crate of wine from one, then another from another. His arms ache but he doesn't complain. He waits for the boss's orders.

Preta returns to her spot at the front of the group. She cocks the shotgun. She moves ahead slowly and the Red Foot move with her.

Preta is positioned at the front of the raft. She's still holding the gun. The craft is five yards by five, jury-rigged from leftover bits of old wood with a small motorboat coupled to the side. It's docked at the improvised, secret port, which they themselves built on the riverbank, on the Argentine side. On the Brazilian side there is another.

They hear the water of the Yucumã Falls in the distance and the furious rush of the current. No one speaks. Totally focused, they communicate only through signals. Preta, apprehensive, looks from side to side. She doesn't like doing this work during the day. The risks are too great, but today the money offered by Enrico and his associates is considerable too. And there's no time to lose.

The group is split: one part on the raft, receiving the merchandise and positioning it in the center; the rest on the shore. They finish loading. Preta turns to the ones on land and gives the signal. The adolescents and the older members of the group quickly run into the woods and hide. Only León stays where he is, watching Preta, escaping her notice. She signals to the man in the small boat, who starts up the motor. The raft begins to move slowly. Preta fixes her eyes on the other side of the river, the small shingle beach, where they will moor to unload the merchandise that the *graxains* — that's what they call the men who come into the Turvo park on motorbikes — will take. From there, having evaded duty, all the contraband will travel to Dourado, then on to Porto Alegre, São Paulo, and in the case of most of the wild animal meat, to Asia.

They hear the sound of another motor. Coming up against the current appear two Navy boats. Ângelo, the head of the park, is at the fore of one, accompanied by soldiers and agents from the environmental brigade. One of the Red Foot draws the revolver from his belt and shoots, striking the metal hull of the craft. A soldier returns fire, hitting him in the forehead, and he drops dead into the water.

"In the river!" Preta commands.

The women and men with her immediately throw themselves into the water and, with some difficulty, manage to swim back to the Argentine side, where they are rescued by their companions on the riverbank. Preta remains alone on the raft, which keeps on moving. Swiftly she raises her rifle and points it at the police officers and shoots. Two of the Red Foot on the shore fire too. Preta ducks down into the little boat that's fastened to the raft. The soldiers shoot back and a firefight ensues. Ângelo is hit. A bullet strikes the fuel tank of Preta's boat, which bursts into flames. The guards take advantage of the situation to shoot up the merchandise too. The bottles of wine explode, the drink pouring out between the wooden boards. The Styrofoam coolers split. The ice and the meat disappear into the water. There is a deafening cry from inside the woods. Then a woman's voice rings out:

"Ay, no! Ay, no! No!"

Then, from that same place, a desperate commotion seems to grow. Preta comes out of her hiding place, shows herself to the authorities, drops her weapon, raises her arms, and shouts:

"Stop! Don't shoot! I know you want me alive."

The shooting stops. The raft quakes, she sees that it's approaching an eddy, ringed about by strong currents. Preta looks down at the cloudy, rough Uruguai River, then throws herself in. It swallows her up and she disappears.

Violet Sky

As night falls, Chaya walks into Thales's house. He's lying on the living-room floor, wearing a tracksuit, stretching his legs. Still in uniform, she collapses on the sofa.

"I thought it kinda weird you and Enrico not mentioning the hydroelectric project at lunch today," Chaya says.

"Didn't want to spoil the family moment, sis. We've had fewer and fewer of those lately."

"Why did she decide to stay in town so many days?"

"Oh, I've hardly spoken to her." Thales gets to his feet and goes over to the kitchen.

"Riiight. . . . Like I'm gonna believe that."

Thales returns, carrying two glasses of water. He hands one to his sister.

"Did Olga say anything to you about the dam?"

"Chaya . . ."

"I could care less if you guys fucked, if you're gonna go on fucking."

"Sis, seriously, the way you still hate her, after all these years, it's way out of proportion. Let the girl be. She's just come here to do her job and she's leaving now."

Thales gulps the water from his glass. Chaya goes on:

"I don't give a shit about Olga, she can go to hell as far as I'm concerned. What I want to know is who in this town — apart from the Riccis — is backing that worm of a deputy and this ridiculous hydroelectric business."

Thales puts his glass down on the bookcase and turns away from Chaya. She gets up.

"OK, I'm gonna go talk to Enrico. I didn't want to go anywhere near his wine smuggling, but since he's still selling to those bastard politicians in Porto Alegre — including Heichma — he'll be able to help me and ask that asshole who's on his side here in Dourado."

"*Don't.*"

Chaya is surprised to hear Thales raise his voice.

"Our dad's real stressed right now," Thales goes on, "and too old to be fighting with you."

"Your dad."

"Here we go . . . he raised you as his daughter."

"*Your* dad."

"He'd rather die than talk to you about his sketchy dealings with the wine. He's been like that since granny Gringa, he's not gonna change now."

"Bro, look, I do love you, OK? And sure, I'm grateful to Enrico and your late mom for everything they did for me, which is why I've kept this pact of silence — let's call it that — with your dad. I can go on not talking to him about the whole contraband thing, but I *will* talk about the hydroelectric dam."

"God, Chaya. You were the greatest gift I ever got in this life, but fuck's sake, enough now. I would die for you, you know that, but not everything revolves around you, the park, and Sarampião. I'm telling you, our dad — because, yeah he's *our* dad — he's not doing too good. I've never seen him like this before, it's like any moment he's gonna lose his shit. Don't make things worse."

"OK, I'll back off, but just one warning: don't *ever* judge or question my concern for the park again, or what Sarampião means to me."

Thales regrets what he said. He was trying to protect his father, and he hurt his sister. But before he is able to speak again, Chaya's phone rings. She answers. Her expression changes.

"What's up?" Thales asks.

"Ângelo's been shot," Chaya replies, already halfway out the door.

"I'll come with."

"Take your car."

Outside she feels a hot wind brushing past her body. Her skin crawls. She glances at the horizon, the sun is setting in the violet sky. She turns the other way and notices, in the distance, an enormous rain cloud approaching. She gets into the truck and starts it up.

Standing on the sidewalk, Thales just freezes looking at the sky, at that color that can hypnotize even those who do occasionally get to see it. The heavy cloud approaching wrenches him from his contemplation. He runs to the garage.

Winds, Storms, Secrets

It's past eight p.m. Olga is lying in bed in her room at the Jaguar Hotel. The windows are open and there's a strong wind blowing in, tossing about clothes, napkins, and pieces of paper off the table. She gets out of bed and walks over to the window. She watches the effects of the gale on the town: leaves, tree branches, dust, plastic bags, trash. Everything in a whirling dance. As she shuts the window, she hears a knock.

"Who is it?"

"Enrico."

She opens the door.

"Evening, Olga."

"Evening, senhor Enrico."

"I wanted a quick word."

"Sure . . ."

"You know this is a family hotel. We're a small town, but we're respectable, we don't like trouble. You're going to have to check out today."

"I don't understand . . ."

"Then let me be frank: Deputy Heichma knows a lot of folks in this town. We know he's a jealous man who doesn't like not getting his way."

Olga feels her face flush and her eyes burning. She never could have imagined that the story Heichma concocted over at the Legislative Assembly could have made it all the way here to Dourado. Almost all the parliamentarians talk big to one another: They invent relationships with young women from the interior of the state, women they consider weak, naïve, defenseless. They make use of their power and the jobs they give these women to perpetrate all sorts of abuses — psychological, material, and often sexual in nature — relying on the impunity that shields politicians and men of power. They've snuffed out the lives, dreams, and futures of so many women that even Olga has lost count. She can see that she'd innocently believed that the lies would surely never travel very far, let alone back to her hometown. And now she feels what she has felt so often back in the city: shame. Like a scrap of torn, dirty old clothing, that's how she sees herself. There's no point telling the truth. The truth is microscopic alongside the lie coming from the mouth of a powerful man.

"Heichma called, senhor? He called you?" she asks, cornered.

"Hey, what you do with the deputy over in the capital's none of my business. I don't care how you people live there."

"*What I do*? You've known me since I was a little girl, senhor Enrico, how can you think so low of me? Heichma is a decrepit, revolting creature . . . he could be my father, my grandfather. . . . How *dare* you say these things?" Olga is screaming, unable to control herself.

"You can shout all you like, Olga, I don't give a damn about you — all I care about is my son. You did something wrong here in Dourado once, you tried to ruin the kid's future and my family's, no one has any idea how hard I had to work to take care of that."

She wants to challenge him, to remind him that she took all the blame, just as he'd demanded at the time. That she'd suffered all the consequences, to keep Thales out of it. That the whole thing still stung, that she continued to put up with what life gives and what it takes, silently and alone. Alone, as always. But she can't. In her head, scenes from the past are spinning. Scenes of her with her parents, devastated, leaving Dourado in the early hours of the morning, running away, expelled from the town. She snaps out of it when she hears Enrico's order echoing down the hotel corridor.

"So yeah, that's right — you're Heichma's whore, that's all you are. You have one hour to gather up your things and go, or I'll toss you out onto the street myself."

Olga drops the folders with the papers about the hydroelectric project into the trunk of the car. The strong wind is blowing the dust hard into her face and her eyes.

"Fuck. All I needed . . ." She doesn't finish her sentence, because a hand grabs her arm and she screams.

"Relax, Olga," says the voice.

She opens one of her eyes with difficulty and sees Thales.

"You're leaving?"

Olga doesn't answer.

Thales continues: "Why?"

"Oh, please. Everyone hates me here, Thales. Let go and leave me be."

"Olga, stop this — you're doing the same thing you did twelve years ago."

"Well, I'm feeling the same I felt that day," she says. "Or actually, even worse."

"But that's all over."

"You don't get it. It'll never be over."

"Please, don't do this. Let's talk. Let's resolve whatever needs to be resolved like adults. We're adults now and we can . . ."

"We can what, Thales? You're going to stand up to your father, are you? You're gonna confess to what actually happened when we were seventeen?"

Thales doesn't answer.

"Yeah, that's what I thought." Olga moves away from behind the car. Thales follows and hugs her. She doesn't move.

"Just don't leave right yet. There's an ugly-looking storm brewing. Don't get onto the road now."

Olga pushes him away and gets into the car.

"You're only ruining things again."

"Good luck with your perfect life here in Dourado, Thales."

Back on Avenida das Viuvinhas, Olga passes the statue of Sarampião. She stops the car and gets out.

"What do you want me to do, huh? What do you want from me? Want me to say that idiot greeting your great-granddaughter says? Fine, I'll say it! *Arrê, Sarampião*."

She moves closer to the statue. As she looks up, a lightning bolt tears through the sky. Then she places her hand on Sarampião's face, and a series of images flash through her mind: Enrico, the police, Thales, Heichma, her father, her mother, and then, finally,

Chaya. She hears the rumble of thunder. The statue shudders. Olga pulls back her hand and runs to the car.

On her way out of the city, she sees the sign on the right-hand side: *Turvo State Park — Nature Conservation Area — 5 km.* She flicks on her turn signal and takes the exit.

Ten p.m. The gale is blowing even more strongly now. Chaya is standing outside the park HQ with Cláudio, Nestor, and two rangers — a woman and a man. Nestor has his right arm in a sling. The tree boughs sway furiously. A shrill chorus of owls, crickets, cicadas, toads. Chaya speaks loud so that everyone can hear:

"We need to get ourselves organized. We know there's at least ten secret ports in the vicinity of the park. Even more of those fucking makeshift rafts. And we're gonna burn the whole lot down."

"Only we do it without waiting for the brigade's help, right? It'll be another six months otherwise." Cláudio is irritated. In a few days he's seen his partner Nestor wounded, now his boss Ângelo nearly got killed. If they don't act now, he might be next.

A lightning bolt flashes on the horizon. A few seconds later, the sound of thunder. In the same moment, a car with raised headlights stops at the gate. The guard comes out of the guardhouse and says:

"Your lights."

The headlights dip. The driver's door opens.

The rangers watch as a shape moves around to the front of the car. It's Olga.

"Can I speak to Chaya Sarampião, please?"

"Park's closed," the guard replies.

Olga spots Chaya not very far away.

"Please, Chaya," she calls out, "just a couple of minutes."

Chaya walks into the wind, her hair flying. She tells the guard to open the gate, and she approaches Olga. The two of them are illuminated only by the half-light from the car and the small lamp on the guardhouse wall.

"Two minutes. I got more serious things to deal with." Chaya crosses her arms and spreads her legs slightly, making her appear shorter than she is.

"I need your help," Olga pleads. Chaya doesn't respond. "I need to talk to him."

"Him?"

"You know . . . Sarampião." Olga points back toward the town. "I need him to forgive me."

Chaya does nothing, but, man, she could kill Olga right now. Her entire body wants to hurl itself onto the journalist. Olga knows it.

"I know! I know, it seems ridiculous. But it's the only thing I can think of doing," Olga insists.

"I don't know what you're up to, but I swear to God if I see you round here again . . ."

"I think Sarampião would want it too. I'm here for him. Please."

Chaya tries to think rationally for a few moments. She moves away, round the other side of the guardhouse. She disappears into the darkness. She comes back with a fistful of red earth which she puts into the journalist's hand.

"Smell that," Chaya tells her.

Olga looks at the earth. She's confused. She rubs it into her hand.

"Smell it."

Olga brings the earth to her nose.

"That's all you're going to get from him. Now, out of my sight."

"Listen: Sarampião made me come talk to you," says Olga.

"I'm going to smash your . . ."

"Just let me finish — please. Since it happened, what happened back then, since I did those terrible things to his statue, my life has just been this whole run of mistakes I haven't been able to put right. I'm trapped in this infinite cycle of traumas. Anxieties, misfortunes that only get worse and worse, and I can't seem to become better, or a bigger person. . . . In our schooldays, I wanted to be this great socially committed journalist, who'd fight for the truth, who'd expose the crimes of the powerful. But coming back here, to this land, turns out I'm the very opposite of what I once dreamed of being." Olga holds back her tears to preserve what little dignity she has left.

Chaya remains cold.

"Well, it takes guts to recognize that your life is in shambles once you've been through something like that," she says.

"So will you help me?"

"You chose to take that path alone," says Chaya, "you'll have to get out of it alone."

"If you won't do it for me, do it for Sarampião."

"You still remember that red earth?" Chaya asks. "That smell?"

Olga shakes her head, ashamed.

"That earth is him, all of this is him." Chaya gestures at the vast forest of the Turvo park.

"Will you let me inside?"

"Your time's up." Chaya turns her back on Olga and walks off toward the park HQ.

"I can help save this place. I know things about the Gran Roncador plant." The journalist plays her trump card.

Chaya stops in her tracks.

"There's a lot wrong with it," Olga continues. "Heichma's mixed up in it and some powerful people from this town too."

"You think I don't know? I want names. Who's involved?"

Another flash of lightning on the horizon.

"I need to get my hands on concrete proof before I expose them. Just telling you won't do you any good. Nor me . . . But I can get that proof."

"If that's true, maybe Sarampião really did send you."

It starts to rain, thick heavy drops. Both women feel them land, wetting their bodies and their faces.

"Why should I believe you?" Chaya asks.

"Because of everything I've just said. And because I've got a lot of reasons for wanting to end every one of those sons of bitches who're a part of this."

Olga runs over to the car and returns holding her phone.

"Will you give me your number? I'm going to the city. Whatever I'm able to get from the office, or from wherever else, I'll bring here and leave it with you. Then you can show me what I need to do to meet Sarampião."

"You stand to lose more than you stand to gain," says Chaya. "You know that, right?"

"No," said Olga, "I have nothing left to lose."

A Washed Body

Nearly midnight. Preta is soaked to the bone. She's limping as she trudges through the dark along the Uruguai riverbank. The rain is getting heavier. She looks at the sky and sees the flash of a lightning-bolt and then pitch black. There is a gash in her right leg; she smashed into a rock while trying to get free of the river current hours earlier. She's in pain and beginning to feel cold, but she doesn't stop. She passes bushes, rocks, pebbles. She slips. Falls. Gets back up. She feels the cut tearing at her skin. She bites her lip to keep from crying out. Turning left, she starts to cross the scrub, toward the Red Foot settlement. Under the heavy rainfall, she glimpses the lights of the oil lamps, from the candles of the houses, and right at the back, the large old shed, with its beaten-earth floor, where her people are gathered. She walks over. A fire is burning at the entrance. She stops beneath the zinc roof. Two women move away. The body of a twelve-year-old boy is stretched out on top of some wooden planks. Preta sees the hole that's been opened in the kid's chest. The blood that flowed from it has dried.

Without Preta's noticing, a little six-year-old girl approaches and takes her hand. She gives a start. The child smiles and passes her a bucket of water and a white cloth. Serenely, she asks:

"Let's, Preta?"

She takes the bucket and the cloth and walks over to the dead boy on the table. Saturday is not over yet.

1996

The Red Earth – The Red Foot

Unanswered Prayer

Preta, only seventeen, looks at the dilapidated cement tomb, crusted in a layer of greenish moss. She's in a faux leather miniskirt, platform boots, a velvet jacket, and black pantyhose at the back of the cemetery in the upper part of a rural community in Corredera Moconá. Her eyes are strikingly made up. She looks at the words — almost erased now — on the stone: _Roscato Sarampião — *1927 †1958_. Not far from Preta, the gravedigger announces that he's finished. Next to him stands her sixty-seven-year-old grandmother, Tédi. Preta walks over to them. They are beside another grave, this one only recently dug. She takes a few twenty-real notes out of her pocket and hands them to the man.

"May your mom rest in peace," he says.

She doesn't reply. She gets a black pen, a Sharpie, and writes on the wooden cross planted in the ground: _Lenara Sarampião._

"You said you weren't gonna come." Preta addresses her grandmother.

"She was my daughter, after all," Tédi replies.

"Well, seeing as you've finally remembered, how about saying a few words?"

"She made a choice, Preta. We all have a choice, even the most fucked-over of women. She chose the needle and that goddamn powder instead of the Red Foot, instead of family." Tédi licks the tips of her index and middle fingers, holds her granddaughter's head, and rubs the makeup from the girl's eyes. "This crap doesn't go with us. Want our group to respect you? Don't go traipsing around looking like a clown."

Tédi takes her granddaughter's hand and they leave. Outside the cemetery, Preta feels a wind on her back. She turns around, but sees nobody.

"What is it, Preta?"

"The wind."

"Ugh, that same old shit! You and your mom. Sarampião died decades ago. And trust me, the man wasn't so good like he'd turn into some kind of saint who shows up manifesting as the wind. Forget him, and that damn surname. And see if you could maybe grow up a bit? Honestly, Preta, to go on believing that garbage . . ." Tédi walks off toward the waiting car.

Preta stretches out one of her arms and opens her hands. Another gust of wind passes through her fingers. She smiles. She speaks quietly so that her grandmother Tédi will not hear her:

"Arrê, Sarampião!"

The Burden of Survival

Saturday morning. Turvo town square. The Avenida das Viuvinhas is closed to through traffic. A crowd fills the road. The city band is playing near the fountain of the Yucumã Falls and, next to it, two large red cloths covering something big. The music comes to an end and the community bursts into applause.

On the improvised stage stand Enrico Romano, aged fifty, and Thales, his six-year-old son, and another five local authorities and politicians. Armin Sarampião, seventy-four, and Chaya Sarampião, six, are right up front, in the audience. Enrico takes the microphone.

"As president of the Dourado Traders' Association, I'd like to say how pleased I am that we — along with the town hall — after years of serious neglect, are handing over to you, the local residents, our beloved Turvo square now revitalized." Applause. He goes on: "And we're also going to have a surprise. . . ." He points at the red cloths.

Chaya beams, waving at Enrico and Thales on the stage. Only Enrico waves back. Armin is moved to see his granddaughter so happy, and silently he prays that the happiness will last, that the cycle of tragedy that has befallen the Sarampião family for decades will end with her generation. Some years ago, Armin's wife, Idalina, was carried off by a late-diagnosed hepatitis. A few years back, Amara, Chaya's mother and Armin's only daughter, had died from a medical error while giving birth to the girl.

Enrico speaks again:

"Senhor Armin and little Chaya, the son and great-granddaughter of our great Sarampião. Please, come a little closer, both of you. I'm sure you'll be moved when you see what we've arranged." Enrico signals for the band to strike up again. Armin stays where he is, Chaya giddily jumps and claps her little hands. Enrico pulls on the red fabric, to reveal a statue. A statue of Sarampião in concrete, which depicts him with his hair down, falling to his neck, his shirt unbuttoned, a flask hanging from his waist and a rifle at his shoulder.

Chaya runs over and hugs the statue.

"Is this great-grandpa? Is it, grandpa, is it him?"

Armin nods.

Enrico pulls away the second cloth and reveals another, smaller statue, this one in wood, of a jaguar baring its teeth. From the crowd come shouts and murmurs, immediately followed by laughter. Someone exclaims:

"It's old Mad Mouth!"

Armin glares at the jaguar statue, then at Enrico. He takes Chaya's hand.

"We've got to go," he says.

"I don't want to!"

"I promise we can come back tomorrow and you can play here all afternoon."

"OK." She kisses Sarampião's statue on its knee, which is as high as she can reach. "See you tomorrow, great-grandpa."

Armin and Chaya leave the ceremony, as a distressed Enrico watches them go.

As Chaya walks beside her grandfather, she mumbles a quiet prayer:

Arrê, old Sarampião
Arrê, Arrê
Oh caboclo, Arrê
Protect the Turvo
Altar place of everything.

"Where'd you learn that?" asks Armin, intrigued.

"Nowhere."

"Chaya . . . who taught them to you?"

She laughs.

"Fine. It was great-grandpa. It was him."

She raises her arms, asking to be carried. Armin picks her up. The girl hugs him and kisses his face. He does the same. In the background, the band plays on.

That afternoon, a man is rowing Preta across the Uruguai in a small boat.

"Wait here," she orders him. "I'll be back in two or three hours."

She takes a taxi to the Dourado town center. She asks the driver to turn into the first residential neighborhood, on the left, after Avenida das Viuvinhas. He pulls up to the sidewalk. Preta pays the driver and gets out. She walks two blocks, to a house on a large plot of land. She crosses the lawn to the back, where she steps inside a huge greenhouse of wood and transparent plastic.

There's an enormous variety of plants, some hanging from hooks, others on the tables, in the cupboards, on the shelves. She walks carefully over to a bench. She picks up two pots from the floor, moving them aside, then settles herself down, hidden behind the leaves of the bushes.

Preta still insists on seeing Chaya whenever she can, even if Tédi has expressly forbidden it out of hatred for Armin, a hatred she made a point of passing on to her granddaughter. Tédi always made it very clear that it was her brother-in-law, Armin, who was responsible for all the bad things that had happened to Roscato and, as a result, to her and Lenara. If Tédi hadn't established the Red Foot back then, neither she nor Preta would have any future at all. "This is the past we inherited," Tédi was always saying, "and we will need to survive in spite of it."

After the Turvo park, the greenhouse is Chaya's favorite place. At the peak of her six-year-old imagination, she tells Preta that Sarampião only ever leaves the park to come here. Preta never doubted her, despite knowing it was Armin who built and takes care of the place, every plant meticulously catalogued with its scientific and popular name and its medicinal properties. Preta herself has memorized a lot already and, also instinctively, has learned to mix one herb with another and make home remedies and teas for the Red Foot. She believes this is a gift that Sarampião left her.

The greenhouse door opens and slams loudly. She shrinks back under the bench and shifts one of the pots in front of her. She hears footsteps approaching, until a small hand pulls the leaves aside.

"Hi Preta!" Chaya smiles.

Preta gets out and hugs her. Chaya, fascinated by her older cousin, hands her a plate with a slice of bread slathered with mulberry jelly and cream and a glass of grape juice.

"I made it for you."

Preta receives the glass of juice and takes a gulp. She takes a bite of the bread.

"It's great. Thanks."

The two girls look at one another affectionately.

"Were you crying?" Chaya asks.

"I'm all good now, little one."

"I can teach you, cuz."

"Teach me what?"

"What it's like not having a mom."

Chaya kisses Preta's cheek.

"It'll all be OK," she tells her.

They hear a voice:

"Again?"

Chaya runs over to hug her grandfather.

"Chaya, what did grandpa tell you about not coming in here on your own?" asks Armin.

"But I'm not on my own, I'm with my cousin."

He looks at Preta, who tries, unsuccessfully, to conceal the tears in her eyes.

"Your mom is at peace now, Preta," says Armin.

"She's not. There's no peace where she's at. I'd best go . . ."

Armin watches that girl, so sad and simultaneously radiating such rage.

"You're turning eighteen soon. We can fix you up with work here in town or somewhere nearby. There's lots of positions in family homes, in a store. . . . You don't need to stay over there, with those people."

"*Those people?* Those people are my family, you wicked old man — how much more do you want me to give up?" Preta tries to get past him to go.

Armin grabs her arm.

"Honestly, child, you're impossible," says Armin. "Please don't talk like that in front of her."

"Let go."

A frightened Chaya positions herself between the two of them, separating them.

"Stop!"

"You'll only end up like your mom," Armin says.

"My mom ended up that way because of you."

"No, Preta, she ended up like that because Tédi and Roscato were shitty parents."

"Son of a bitch . . . talk about my grandpa and grandma like that again, I'll kill you. I'll put a bullet right here." She sticks a finger in the middle of Armin's forehead.

Armin slaps his great-niece. Preta loses her balance, but recovers and throws herself onto him, and he shoves her away. She falls onto a table covered in pots.

"Come anywhere near Chaya again, I'll call child services on you and the police on Tédi, you just see if I don't," Armin threatens.

"Stop it, grandpa. Stop, Preta," Chaya entreats them.

Preta throws a pot at Armin. It hits his head and he falls, stunned. Impassive, she walks over to her great-uncle. She takes another pot and drops it on the fallen man's face. Chaya screams. There's blood running over the floor. Preta flees.

Enrico appears from the backyard of the house. He wants to apologize to Armin. He never imagined that anybody could connect that wooden jaguar to Mad Mouth, let alone be offended by it. Preta rushes past him, but before Enrico is able to ask her anything, he hears Chaya. He runs to the greenhouse. The girl is kneeling in a puddle of blood, clinging to her grandfather's arm.

"Wake up, grandpa! Wake up! Wake up!"

Fire

A Victory Preordained

A few days after the encounter that got her boss shot, Chaya visits the hospital. She walks past reception, climbs the stairs, and in the hallway, pauses outside room 23, next to the nurses' station. She's overcome by a strange smell, which transports her back to some uncomfortable place, deep inside a painful memory. She recalls her grandfather, the old man crying like a child, with a single feeling, as he sat in a chair at the side of the bed. The bandaged head, the blood-darkened urine pooled on the floor. She fights off the familiar hurt and pain that rush in. She walks on to room 46. Knocks. Opens the door.

"Good morning!"

Ângelo is in bed. He's sleeping. There's an oxygen machine on the right connecting to tubes inserted into his nose. On the left, the saline drips slowly. Cláudio and Nestor, the latter with his arm still in a sling, stand near the window. A woman rises from the armchair right by the door, getting up to greet Chaya.

"Hi — I'm Dinorá, Ângelo's wife." She holds out her hand.

"Chaya. Chaya Sarampião. I work with him."

"Thanks for coming."

Ângelo wakes up and with some difficulty manages to open his eyes. Cláudio and Nestor notice and approach the bed.

"I'll go tell the nurse he's up. You three stay and chat." Dinorá walks to the door, and before leaving, flashes a look of concern at Ângelo.

"This time I really thought I was going to . . ." says Ângelo, effortfully, and he points at the gunshot wound almost in his chest, below his right shoulder.

"You did give us a fright, senhor Ângelo," agrees Cláudio.

"Yeah. I wasn't as lucky as Nestor."

Nestor smiles tight-lipped and turns toward the window that overlooks the courtyard and the hospital car park, trying not to show how profoundly he hates seeing a colleague in that condition.

Chaya doesn't take her eyes from the oxygen tubes attached to Ângelo's nostrils. He lies motionless in the bed, his abdomen swathed in dressing, deep bags under his eyes, his lips bruised and cracked. *Fragile*, she thinks. He doesn't look like that unwavering man, that irritable boss, who never has a kind word for anyone, who never bothers to hide the rage built up over months on the job, in a place that Chaya knows full well he detests. They'd butted heads since the first field trip they took together in the park. But at no point did they argue over power, only territory, as Chaya said. And deep down, this was what he most respected and admired in her. She understands the reserve, its regular visitors, its fauna and flora, better than anyone. Ângelo needs her for his own career to work out. And the one time he did something without consulting Chaya, because he was furious with his subordinate for letting that Argentine boy go, this gunshot was the result.

Ângelo gestures for Chaya to move closer. She doesn't respond. Cláudio touches her back lightly and nudges her gently toward the boss.

"I asked you all to come because it's going to take me some time to recover," Ângelo says. "I've got to have someone in my place," and he brings his hand to his dry mouth. He tries to reach for the glass with water and a straw on the side table near the foot of the bed, but he can't do it.

Cláudio hands him the glass; he takes a couple of gulps with some difficulty.

"Chaya, you're standing in for me temporarily, you're in charge of the park," says Ângelo.

Cláudio looks with some confusion at Ângelo, then at Chaya.

"I don't want anybody questioning my decision." Ângelo is firm, his voice as loud as he can manage.

Chaya can see there's something in Ângelo's eyes that goes beyond the pain he's feeling from the injury. There's fear.

"I've notified SEMA already. Chaya, you know what to do, soldier — men, you're to follow her orders, no questions."

The three of them stand there, arms behind their backs, legs apart, heads lowered.

"You're dismissed."

"Yes, sir," say Nestor and Cláudio in unison.

The two men leave. Chaya looks at the floor for a couple of seconds. She says nothing. Then she turns to leave, but at the door, stops.

"Get better soon, boss."

"Don't do anything too stupid," says Ângelo.

"I'll try my best." She shuts the door.

In the hallway, she stops once again at the door to room 23. Impulsively she turns the handle. The iron bed is still at the right of the room. A small sink at the back and, beside it, a single-door cupboard with drawers. The morning sunlight peeps timidly through the blinds. On the left, a chair with a wooden seat. She sits down and falls silent.

I so wish you were here. You'd be proud now. Your granddaughter — the granddaughter of an ex-dairyman, great-granddaughter of Sarampião: head of the Turvo park. OK, interim head, but still head. Sorry I haven't been back here, or to the cemetery. It's just, the way we said goodbye was so hard, grandpa. I didn't want to let you go — you know, just one of those little kid things, not understanding how life works, let alone death. The way you were crying. I couldn't handle it. I felt guilty. That feeling of fragility, of innocence that ended up being lost. I just left the room and hid. It took me years to understand that you weren't crying from pain, but from sorrow, because you knew you had to go and you didn't want to leave me here alone. Alone in this world. Alone just like Pretu would end up too. You should know, Grandpa Armin, I'm doing everything within my power to keep Sarampião's place well protected. But you do know it, of course. Wherever you are, you know.

She gets up. She looks around at the walls of the room and feels the tears coming, uncontrollable. She takes a deep breath, gets a tight grip on that feeling of helplessness that always assails her thoughts when she's in this hospital. Then she wipes her wet face, leaves the room, goes down the stairs. At reception, she bumps into Enrico Romano.

He sees the melancholy in her expression.

"Chaya, my dear."

"Good morning." She tries to hide it.

"How's the lieutenant?"

"He's woken up."

"A tragedy." He hugs her affectionately.

"However much we try, we're never ready for something like this," she says.

"You're right. But you don't need to go through it alone. Come back home, stay there a bit with me and Thales."

She removes herself from his hug and says:

"I've got to go on shift at the park. There's nobody else."

"But they'll send more people to help, right? I guess he'll be off for some time?"

"Yeah."

"Do they know yet who's taking his place?"

"Me. . . . It'll be me, just temporarily."

Enrico's face breaks into a smile.

"I'm so proud," he says. "So very proud. No one is more qualified, better prepared, better suited to the role than you, my child."

"Chaya. Just call me Chaya."

"Please, at least at moments like this allow me to call you my child! My daughter! Your grandpa Armin would be celebrating now."

Chaya's expression darkens. She makes for the exit. Enrico is taken aback.

"Chaya?"

"Sorry, got so much stuff to do over in the park."

Enrico climbs the stairs, walks the hallways, stops outside room 46. He knocks and enters.

Ângelo is not surprised to see him.

"A good day, buddy?" says Enrico.

"It's done," Ângelo tells him quietly.

Enrico comes over to the bed. He rests his hand on the pale police officer, so hurt and vulnerable. After the trauma of what's happened to him, no one can be sure whether he'll ever be able to return to fieldwork.

Dinorá reappears.

"What're you doing here?" she asks.

"I just stopped by to wish him a speedy recovery."

Enrico looks at Ângelo, then at Dinorá, and leaves.

Too Near to the Problem, Too Far from the Solution

October 29. Tuesday night. Olga and Heichma are at a restaurant. Heichma's eyes never leave her breasts, and — quite indifferent to the surrounding conversations, the laughter, the clinking of cutlery against plates — he chews a piece of rare picanha steak with his mouth open. Then he guzzles red wine from a fat-smeared glass. Olga looks at her own dish, which has remained untouched since it was served.

The waiter approaches.

"Let's have a glass of your Uruguayan now, my friend," says Heichma.

The waiter nods and leaves.

With the tip of his shoe, Heichma nudges Olga's shin under the table. She looks at that repulsive figure opposite, and her sole reaction is to scoot her chair back.

"So the president of TVE still hasn't given you an exact date?" she continues.

"I've already said. Relax, woman. You're always trying to run before you can walk. There's no point trying to trample over me. If you only made a bit more of an effort . . ." he said, and his eyes return to Olga's breasts, allowing the meaning behind his words to be clearly understood. He drinks the rest of his wine. Burps. He takes the bottle and tops her off with what's left. He sets the empty to one side.

"Drink," he says.

She takes a sip.

"It's been two years since I passed the public service exam, they've already filled all sorts of other positions at TVE, there's only my reporter job missing, and no sign of the guy actually signing off my name for an announcement in the Gazette. It's like he's just toying with you, belittling you, seeing as after all — like you say — you've asked him so many times already. You must think it's kind of strange?"

"Fuck's sake!" he roars.

The people at the next table turn to look.

"No need to shout."

He lowers his voice. "Look, you're talking crap, OK? You think it's easy? I've told you, the man owes me. A lot of people in the party owe me, him especially. It's a matter of time. Trust in your deputy, little Olguinha," he says, and rubs his shoe on her leg, hurting her shin. She kicks him away and moves even further back.

"Oh don' you be tryin to get away now . . ." laughs Heichma, putting on a rustic accent.

The waiter arrives with another bottle of wine. Before opening it, he shows the label to the deputy, who puts on his glasses and reads it with care. In that same moment, Olga picks up her own glass of wine, discreetly, and tips the liquid into a plant pot beside the table. The waiter sees, but gives no reaction at all. He removes the cork and pours for them both.

"I'm going to need to keep my whole salary this month," says Olga.

"I don't want to talk about that now."

"Actually, I'll need to keep my whole salary up till the end of the year."

"You know that's not possible." He grits his small dark teeth, then puffs out some hot stale-smelling breath.

"It's only a few months. I'm late on the installments for my car."

"Your father and mother have good pensions. Ask them."

Olga feels her hands and legs trembling and her back burning.

"You want me to ask my parents for money because I only get to keep half of my own salary, half the salary that's actually on my payslip? Since I've got to take the other half and hand-deliver it right to you? Senna gets to keep his whole salary, and the guy's been here less time than me."

"Are you crazy? You don't *hand-deliver* anything to me. What's gotten into you? Why are you bringing this up now? Here in public? What are you hoping to achieve?" He looks to one side and then the other, suspicious. "You're eating good meat, drinking fine wine. Don't ruin it." Heichma takes Olga's hand, she tries to free herself, but he holds on tight.

"It's *my* salary that's paying the check here," she snaps, confronting him, still trying to free herself.

Heichma lets go of her and slams his fist down on the table.

"This is why you'll never make anything of yourself," he says. "Nothing!"

She looks right at him, but doesn't answer.

"You're on such a short fuse," he says, "and you're impatient, and stupid. Three things most women are these days. Only a few are lucky enough to have a good man to set them straight. Being a good guy, I want to help you, but you don't let me! You don't want my help, because you're stupid. You think you're going to be young and beautiful forever?"

Olga feels her heart racing. If she was braver, she'd take a knife and stick it in his neck right here. She sees people at nearby tables watching them. Whispering. She needs to pull herself together.

"I'm going to the bathroom."

"Wait," he lowers his voice. "*Fine.* I'll talk to Senna. But promise to drop all this. Let's have a laugh and drink some nice wine until the restaurant closes. Deal?"

Heichma pours some more wine and raises his glass to toast.

"To blessed money. Which helps and hinders in equal measure."

Olga waits a moment before raising her glass and taking a sip.

"If the Gran Roncador project pans out over in Dourado," he says, "there's going to be so much money, I mean *so* much money, that I'll pay every installment on your car and the two of us can go traveling round Europe together. And don't you start coming up with excuses."

Olga feels the acrid wine trickle down her throat. She retches, but forces it down.

"That hydroelectric project really does sound like a real river of money." She straightens out her jacket and tosses her hair back.

"Bigger than the Uruguai. The Gran Roncador is going to make me rich, and it's going to line the pockets of the businessmen, of all those fucking politicians up in Brasília, and in Argentina, for generations to come," he pronounces, slurring his words.

"I can't help but wonder — how can such a big project have so much money to spare?"

"That's more like it! A dumb woman trying to learn! Well, it's like with your salaries. Part of them goes to the office, right? A contribution, a bit of payback for everything I've done and I do for each of you. Same for whoever's going to build the plant," he said.

"But the tender process isn't the same as the wages of employees in positions of trust," Olga leads, hoping he will divulge more.

"Oh, no. It's much bigger. And they're going to give me a cut for having opened the tap of this public money for them."

"Congrats, Deputy Heichma. How very clever of you."

He tries to run his hand over Olga's hair, but she recoils, preventing him from coming close. Heichma laughs, he find this amusing, still believing this to be something like a game. Olga picks up her purse from the seat beside her.

"I really do need to go to the bathroom."

"What do you need your purse for?"

"I'm on my period, Deputy Heichma," she says loudly.

"*Please*, keep that to yourself. You're like my wife! For God's sake, some things you shouldn't talk about in public."

Olga squeezes the tampon between her fingers. She heads toward the bathroom and steps inside. Locking the door behind her, she pulls out her phone from the inside pocket of her jacket. The recorder is still running. She presses PAUSE, then saves the file. Playing it back, she listens for a few seconds just to be sure that it has recorded and that the sound quality is good. She opens the bathroom door, and before leaving, she checks that Heichma is distracted. Head lowered, she hugs the wall behind the tables at the back and escapes through the doorway to the kitchen. The staff are surprised. She asks where the exit is. The only woman among them points to a gray door. Olga thanks her and goes through the door, which was already ajar. Then she runs as fast as she can, disappearing into the darkness of the deserted street.

The next morning, at 7:30, Olga is first to the office. She locks the door, careful to leave the key half-turned in the keyhole, making it impossible for anyone to open from outside without forcing it. She drops her purse and coat onto the table before lighting a cigarette. Wandering over to Senna's small office, she opens the cupboard, rummages around the boxes, folders, and papers, searching for the accounting ledger he keeps there. With the cigarette clamped between her lips, she sits down in the chair, taking a good look around the desk and trying to open the left-hand drawers. Locked. She tries the ones on the right. Locked. She hears the main office door lock being forced until the door opens. She gets up. Even with that strategy she'd devised to buy her a few more seconds, she's still alarmed. She takes the cigarette from her mouth. Senna appears.

"Morning," he says, suspicious.

"Morning. Aren't you quite the early bird?" Olga takes another drag.

She goes over to the window and opens it. An icy wind rushes in.

"What are you doing in here?" he asks.

"It's the smokehouse, isn't it!"

Senna does not like this answer, despite having been the person who gave his office the nickname.

"What are you doing here so early?"

"Just wanted to get ahead on a few things. I want to be out by four today."

She puts out what's left of the cigarette on the ashtray on the desk in front of her.

"You still haven't handed over last month's money," Senna says.

"I talked to the deputy yesterday."

"And I talked to him today."

Olga stops, saying nothing for a moment.

"Fine, I'll do a transfer."

"You want to reinvent the wheel now? You know it's cash, in an envelope."

"Fucking hell, you don't exactly make things easy. I'll go to the bank at lunchtime and wait in line to get this shit done." Olga strides out of the room.

Midday. The only people in today are Olga, Senna, and Ana Paula. Senna comes out of his office and walks past his secretary, informing her that he's off for lunch.

"Deputy not coming in today?" probes Olga.

"Meeting off-site," Senna replies.

Olga knows this for a lie. She has access to Heichma's calendar. He must have drunk himself to sleep sitting at that restaurant table, as he'd done so many times before. Olga goes into Senna's room and pushes the door open. Well past fearing repercussions, she takes a screwdriver from a tool kit gifted to the deputy from a wholesaler well known in the state, which the chief of staff keeps in his cupboard for emergencies. Using all her strength, she breaks open one of the desk drawers. There's no way she'll be able to disguise that.

Best to be quick, before Senna comes back. She finds the notebook listing all the “rachadinhas” transferring portions of the employees’ wages for the past four years. She has no idea who some of these names are. Ghost employees. She gets her phone and snaps photos. On the last pages of the notebook: names of businessmen, dates, places, and sums. A separate list on the next page with the words “*Brasília — Ministries*,” and the acronyms of parties that make up the current government.

She documents everything. Then she leaves quickly and runs into Ana Paula.

“You didn’t see anything.”

Olga enters Heichma’s office next, but before shutting the door, she freezes. What is she doing? What if somebody appears and catches her taking — no, stealing — this evidence? She goes back to the secretary:

“Listen, Ana Paula, I need your help. Please. Let me know if anybody’s coming, OK? Either one of them.”

Ana Paula doesn’t move.

“Ana Paula, look,” Olga is practically shouting, “they’ll kill me if they find me in here. And I do mean *literally*. You understand?”

The secretary moves her lips and murmurs: “Yes.”

Olga closes the door, repeating to herself: “They’re going to kill me. What am I doing? They’re going to kill me. . . .” An imaginary siren is blaring inside her. Mustn’t panic. She can’t back out now. She’s got to think fast. She goes straight to the safe and tries a code. Nothing. She tries again. Nothing. She goes over to the private laptop that Heichma forgot on his desk last night, leaving in a hurry to meet her at the restaurant. She turns it on, keys in the same code. Error. She tries his candidacy number. The screen opens up. She looks for incriminating files but finds nothing. Her hands are shaking. Her legs are shaking. Anxiety and fear have overtaken her entire body.

"Easy, Olga, take it easy," she says to herself.

She returns to the safe. One last try. She uses the same code from the laptop. It works.

"Christ, how did this moron ever get to be a deputy?"

Inside the safe, she finds pre-contracts with the logo and name of the Gran Roncador Binational Consortium and a construction firm called SAMDD, based in Canoas, a metropolitan region of greater Porto Alegre. Handwritten in pencil beside each phase of future construction are the names of politicians and businessmen from Dourado, including Enrico Romano, Maurício and Claudenir Ricci, and also Heichma's name and that of other politicians from Rio Grande do Sul and Brasília, as well as ministers from the current federal government, along with numbers corresponding to sums of money in reals. She takes them all out to photograph. And that's when she sees, at the back of the safe, a plastic bag with a USB drive inside. She connects it to the deputy's computer. There are various folders with files and Excel spreadsheets named "Gran Roncador," containing both the actual and deliberately overpriced values for each phase of the project and, beside them, the percentages and names of their relevant beneficiaries. Again, the names of businessmen and firms from across the country, the names of politicians and aides linked to the federal government and the current president of the Republic. A real bomb, Olga tells herself. Ana Paula appears.

"Senna's in the hall talking to Deputy Camargo's press officer," she says.

“God, I’m so screwed! And I still haven’t been able to take photos of everything.”

“I’ll figure something out.” Ana Paula says and hurries off.

Olga still needs to photograph those documents. She won’t have time to send herself the files from the drive, there are just too many. She puts it in her pants pocket. She takes photos of the whole pile of paperwork then returns everything to where she’d gotten it from. Then she notices, inside the safe but on one side, camouflaged, a black envelope, labeled STATEMENTS. It contains a number of bank statements from two savings accounts of Senna’s and one in the name of Alaíse Maria Heichma, the deputy’s wife. There are records of receipt for hundreds of deposits of up to 2,000 reals made in cash over the past four years.

Ana Paula reappears. She stands there in a strange silence, chewing on her lower lip.

“What’s happened? Where is he?” Olga whispers.

“He’s gone down to the speaker’s office. I told him they’d called saying there was someone there from Brasília waiting to see the deputy. He *ran* to the elevator.”

Olga smiles at her, sharing their complicity.

“Thank you. Not long now. I’ll be quick.”

The secretary returns to her desk, taking a few dirty crumpled pieces of folded paper from her drawer.

Olga closes the safe and runs to her desk, picks up her purse and coat. Before she leaves, Ana Paula puts the papers in her hand.

“What’s this?” asks Olga, surprised.

“It’s the deputy’s phone bills, showing the calls made to and from his private cell phone the last few months.”

“How did you get these?”

"Well, you know . . ."

"I don't. Spill."

"He asked me to disable the mailbox on his phone and the idiots at the phone company enabled the printed-out bills."

"Has Heichma seen these?"

"I haven't shown them to him, I'm not crazy. If they're any help with whatever you're doing, use them. I want to see that pig in jail too," she says, like a person expelling something repellent that they've long had trapped inside them.

"I'm going to finish that son of a bitch. You should quit. Get out of here while there's still time," Olga says quickly, headed for the door.

"No, I'm gonna watch from a ringside seat, Olga. Only don't let me down."

Olga goes along the hallway, past the restrooms, turns right, arrives at the fire door opposite the service elevators, and runs down the nine flights of stairs.

Jaguar Blood

October 30. Afternoon. Preta is standing in the middle of the dry, sparse grass. Around her, the terrain is dotted with the houses and containers that make up the small settlement of the Red Foot. She's wearing shorts, a tight tank top with no bra, and flat leather sandals. Her long black hair falls down to her hips. Fixed to her right leg, a bandage over the gash that she got at the police raid on the Uruguai. Women, men, the elderly, adolescents, and children surround her. Only León stands back, head lowered and arms crossed.

"They slaughter us like pigs," Preta yells, "like some kind of vermin, and now that we attack, when we defend ourselves, what do they call us? Animals!" She approaches a middle-aged woman with a haggard face, dirty hair tied with a bit of string, sitting on a stump under a tree, trying to escape the harsh sun. Preta helps her to her feet.

"Kerenne, your mourning time is over." She looks to the others. "They killed her boy and robbed us of our livelihood. The money has turned into blood. And for what?"

A man walks over to where the two women are standing.

"Because they want to control us, Preta. To oppress people through total grim poverty. I came over from the other side of the river, like you. And you know, even our poverty turns them a great profit," says José.

"That's right, my friend. They want us to live according to the laws they've devised, then they themselves break the greatest law of all: Do not kill children. *No matar los niños.* We're not gonna take it. They think they're in the right, but the right will always be on the side of whoever is struggling to eat and to stay alive."

Preta hugs Kerenne tight and declares, loudly so that everyone can hear:

"We shall not let them pass!"

Shouts and whistles. People lift their clenched fists.

"Red Foot! Red Foot!"

León, still at some distance from the rest, is the only one not to raise his voice.

With a gesture, Preta silences the group.

"We have suffered a terrible loss. They take from us, we will take from them. Ready your weapons," Preta orders, "and the tarps, the rock salt, and the ice. And the kerosene and gas too."

"Are we all going?" asks José.

"Only the adults."

José looks straight at Preta and respectfully summons the courage to ask:

"What exactly will you want us to do, boss?"

"Tonight we're going into the Turvo and we'll camp there. And we're not leaving till we've got ourselves a jaguar."

All eyes are on Preta now, disbelieving and scared. She's never allowed a jaguar to be killed before. It was always the one game in the Turvo that was expressly forbidden. Everybody knows that any hunter who did that was under penalty of death from her. A few years ago, one of those people fled on the Uruguai and his body was found months later, eaten by palometas. She looks at her group, and she knows what it is they're feeling. But it's a fear that no words can alleviate — she needs to go beyond what is spoken, beyond what is visible. Preta knows what must be done. She notices León approaching, and she doesn't like what she sees: a cold fixed smile, a disturbing expression.

Preta sits alone on a rock, her bare feet sinking in the damp burgundy mud of the riverbank. She feels the chill of the earth cooling the soles of her feet and between her toes, a balm for the hot afternoon air. She looks up at the woods of the Turvo park over on the other side of the Uruguai. She shuts her eyes, focuses on the sounds of the water.

"Will you give me a sign?" she asks out loud.

She stretches her arms out to her sides, splays her fingers.

"Just a sign. Arr . . . Saram . . . I can't speak those lines again if no one's listening. Have you abandoned me, great-grandpa?"

Suddenly the wind dies and time seems to stop. Everything suspended, as if waiting for an announcement that the very same tragedy was about to recommence. The cycle that is never complete. The continuing parade of blood and death. The gunshot and the jaguar's growl echoing across that place once again.

Preta gets up, turns to go into the scrubland, back to the Red Foot. She hears the motor of a boat. It's Enrico approaching on a small craft, alone. He pulls in close to the riverbank, but doesn't disembark.

"All done," he tells her.

Preta looks at him.

"I know."

"When do you people go?" Enrico asks.

"That's not your concern."

"I need the merchandise, Preta. There's a shipment leaving the port of Rio Grande at the end of the week."

"You don't just rush a hunt like this. Not with this animal. Even your idiot brother would have known that, if we was alive," says Preta.

"May God forgive you for all the cruelty that comes out that mouth of yours."

"God doesn't come this side of the river, old man." Preta turns her back on Enrico and is gone.

Ruining Somebody's Life

That same afternoon, Olga is in her car, headed west on the BR-386. The sun is beating down hard on the windshield and she puts on her shades. She's just passing through the town of Estrela when her phone rings. It's her father.

"*I've never met anyone who tries so hard to ruin their own life as you do, Olga*," he says on the other end of the line.

"Hi, Dad. I'm fine, thanks. How are you guys?"

"*Heichma's called me three times already. Senna's called me ten, maybe fifteen. Where are you?*"

"I'm chasing after my freedom."

"*You're coming adrift, that's what you're doing. You spend so much time looking for that so-called freedom of yours, there'll come a point when you won't know where to look for a future anymore, child.*"

"OK, Dad, cool! With you in my corner I'm feeling so much better already. Want my advice? Stop answering their calls! And it'd be good for you guys to get the car and go to Goiás, to Tia Cristina's for a bit."

"*No! We're coming for you. So tell me: Where are you?*"

"Listen: I know what I'm doing, I'm going to end all those men who've tried to ruin my life. So keep your distance. And stop answering the phone!"

"*I'll come fetch you, and we can go talk to Heichma together. Return all the crap you stole. Save that job and skin of yours.*"

"You really haven't understood a word I'm saying. Amazing . . ."

"*What's amazing?*" he interrupts her.

"Whenever we're talking about what's best for me, we're always on opposing sides."

Olga hears a sigh from the other end of the line, followed by a silence, a very common occurrence between her and her father.

"There's no going back, dad. I'm going to settle some debts in Dourado, and from there I'm going to Argentina. Now, seeing as you called to give me a hard time, best for you and Mom to know that things could get a bit dicey for me for a little while. Which is why I've got to get out of Brazil. I can't give you details down the phone."

"*Why can't you talk on the phone?*"

"Bugged — well, I mean, if it isn't yet, it will be by the end of the day."

"*This whole thing is ridiculous. We're coming to Dourado to find you.*"

"I've already told you I'm going into hiding."

"*Then we can all be hidden together.*"

"No. It's not what I want."

"*It's my fault,*" he lets out a sob, then begins to cry.

Olga takes the phone from her ear and holds it away from her face. With her other hand, the one holding the steering wheel, she gives the dashboard a blow, then another, then resumes her hold on the wheel. For a moment, her whole life flashes before her eyes. It's too much to deal with. Even if it's her father's remorse, for which she has waited so long. A father and a mother untouched by any suffering on her part. Consciously absent. She brings the phone back to her ear.

"I kept myself blind on purpose, kid — I didn't understand any of it, none of what's been going on since we left Dourado, or what was happening to you in Porto Alegre. Stupid, cruel punishment for us and for you after what you did when you were a teenager. We've all lost," he goes on.

Olga still hasn't said anything, and for a moment she considers asking him and her mother to stay where they are, where they've always been. Totally removed from the hell her life has become in the hands of that politician friend of the family, a guy in whom her parents naïvely — even to this day — place total trust. Ask them to stay far away, in their proper place, a place of ignorance, absence, complacence.

"Yeah, we've all lost," she echoes, before saying, firmly: "But we can start over. Listen, go over to the Misiones province in Argentina, it's closer for you guys. Wait for me at some hotel there. When I'm in Argentine territory, I'll tell you where to meet me. I've already got another phone and a new number. I'll give it to you later," and she hangs up without saying goodbye.

Olga parks by a gas station. There are no trees around, the ground is dried earth, light brown, and no customers to be seen; it's like a desert here in the west of Rio Grande do Sul. One solitary attendant perches on a wooden stool between two pumps. Olga takes a black smartphone, an older model, out of her pocket and checks that the transfer is complete. She goes through picture by picture in turn, each file that she photographed in the deputy's office that morning. It's all there. She presses play on the recording she made the previous night. It's safe. She takes her own cell phone and, using a paperclip to eject the SIM tray, she removes the card. Then she gets out of the car holding the card in one hand and the silver phone in the other, and walks over to the attendant, who is still sitting on his stool.

"Have you got a vat someplace for dumping used oil?"

"You can give it to me, I can take it," the pump attendant offers, without getting up.

"Nah, don't trouble yourself, amigo. Just tell me where it is."

"Turn around. You'll see it — right there at the back."

She crosses the hot asphalt. The smell of diesel, gas, and burned rubber fills her nostrils, carried on a stifling wind. She sees the rusty metal tank with a blue plastic lid, next to a brick building with two toilets. On the door of one of them, the letter M, on the other an F, both painted in yellow. Olga lifts the plastic lid off the tank, throws in the SIM, followed a few seconds later by the phone. They sink into the dark, thick liquid and disappear.

Iron, Fire, and Earth

The flames color the naked bodies of the Red Foot women and men who encircle the tall bonfire. Preta appears — naked too, besides a piece of cloth wrapped around her wounded leg. She walks past the others till she is in the center, beside the fire. Then two adolescent boys appear, one wearing a lilac-colored tank top, the other a brown T-shirt, both in shorts and with Havaianas on their feet. Between them, they are carrying a pot full of water and assorted leaves. Preta, looking very focused, casts her eyes around at all those present. The boy in the lilac tank top hands her a metal cup. She fills it with liquid from the pot, then heads over to one of the women in the group and pours the greenish-brown leafy water over her head and body. The woman gasps. The water is icy. Preta repeats the ritual with each person, and finally with herself. She lifts her arm to reveal a scar made with a branding iron, encrusted in her skin, in an *R* shape with a line slicing the letter in half. It's between her ribs, under her armpit.

"This mark protects me, it protects my soul and my body, just as it protected my grandmother Tédi when she founded the Red Foot."

Everybody looks at Preta, fascinated.

"Tédi gave me her most precious belonging," she says as she runs her hand over the scar, "and I'm going to share it with all of you, because what we're about to do inside that forest is also gonna mess with things that we cannot see. But each person who comes with me on the hunt will have their skin and their spirit sealed, just like mine."

The mesmerizing effect that Preta's mark has on everybody overcomes any lingering fear. They trust their leader, but they trust the legend of the mark even more. Until now, many weren't even sure it existed.

The adolescent in the brown T-shirt passes an open bottle of wine to their leader. She drinks.

"Stand in a line," Preta instructs them, pointing forward.

They do as they've been told. Preta looks at the boy in the lilac-colored top, who pulls a knife out of a leather sheath and hands it to her. She takes another gulp of wine and shuts her eyes, then makes a small cut just below her scar. The first woman approaches, Preta dips her fingers in the blood that's running down the side of her body and smears it on the woman's face, before handing her the bottle of wine.

"Have faith! Go on, girl, be strong!"

An hour later, the Red Foot are all gathered in the big old shed that doubles as a storehouse, not far from the group's houses and containers. They're wearing shirts, long pants, and jackets in a dark color or camo print. Some are in boots, others in sneakers.

A group of men is hard at work, hauling coolers with sealed bags of ice. Two of them, up in their years but tall and strong, their long gray hair tied with a leather strap, convey sacks of rock salt to the front, beside the tarps that will be used for tents, and the blankets, hammocks, wooden planks, rifles, revolvers, knives, machetes, and gallons of gasoline and kerosene.

León, standing amid the adults, doesn't take his eyes off the weapons. He's never seen so many in one place. He had no idea Preta had a whole arsenal in her power. She watches him. She approaches the adolescent and takes his arm, leading him to the only table, where two women are organizing ammo for the arms. She gets everybody's attention.

"Once we're on the other side, we're gonna split up. A bigger group will go to the western tip then head south, skirting the edge of the park. They'll set fire to the scrub on that side." Preta takes a piece of paper out from her shirt — she's drawn a map on it. "This will drive the jaguar and the rest of the animals in the other direction, toward the river, where we're gonna be set up."

León picks up a pistol. Immediately, Preta grabs his fist and squeezes till he lets go. A chilling expression crosses his face again.

"León will be the only adolescent to go with you, the rest will stay behind in Red Foot. He'll go with the fire group as he's quick on his legs, quickest of any of us. We need him to warn us if anything goes wrong," Preta says.

"No!" He breaks free from Preta's grip. She cuffs his ear. The boy still tries to argue.

"You're needin me to kill la onça, the jaguar."

Preta grabs him by the collar and drags him out of the big shed.

"So you want a weapon, is that it, asshole? You want to kill? I'm gonna fucking skin you alive. I'm in charge here and you'll do as I say. You know, I once even thought you could be a leader someday . . . but you just think with your balls same as all men. Learn to use this." Preta taps on his forehead with her index finger.

"Sí señora."

The two of them go back into the shed.

"León, help them carry the gasoline and kerosene," Preta orders. Then she turns to the others. "Everyone good to go? Red Foot!"

"Red Foot! Red Foot!" they chant.

Preta gets her pistol, sticks it into her waistband, then takes a .44 rifle, checks the ammo. Then she looks out into the pitch dark, dazed by the awareness that she will never be the same after what she's about to do.

An Ember That Should Never Have Been Lit

It is still the night of October 30. Chaya and Thales are standing on the sidewalk outside his house. In her dirty, damp uniform and her muddy combats, Chaya feels a tiredness she doesn't remember feeling since she first began as a ranger. She's spent more than a day scouring the park for the hidden ports and rafts of the Red Foot. She's irritated, frustrated. Ever since she took over as interim head of the team, and precisely because the post was only interim, she has been thwarted at every turn. They didn't even let her have a patrol from the environmental brigade to work alongside her on the search. Her head is spinning from so many things that need doing, all the paperwork she needs to fill out before she can go to bed. But here she is at Thales's, because he called her for an urgent chat about Enrico.

"Look, I'm going, Thales. You made such a fuss on the phone, I thought this was about Enrico, but so far you've only talked about her." Chaya heads back to the truck, parked across the road, and Thales follows.

"But it *is* about dad . . . and about her too . . . and about you. I don't want you pissed with me again now, sis."

"You already know what I think, Thales, so why even ask me?"

"Could you try to put yourself in my shoes?"

"I'm not thinking about this," Chaya says brusquely. "No. No, I couldn't."

"Course not. You really *can't* understand how I feel at all. You're right, it was a terrible idea. Goodnight, Chaya." He walks back toward his house.

"Stop — what do you mean?" Chaya asks.

"I only wanted you to help."

"What do you mean?"

"You know . . . You've never been in a relationship. You've never been in love with somebody for years the way I have with Olga."

Despite having been raised by Thales's father and mother since she was seven, Chaya has needed to hold on tight, deep inside, to being a part of the Sarampião family. When she was little she used to tell herself every day that she was not a Romano but a Sarampião, almost like a mantra. Thales was the only one who didn't act like he felt sorry for her, never pitied the poor orphan girl. He treated her the way a brother treats a sister. Not reminding her constantly that her blood family was a family doomed to tragedy and that she was, in reality, alone in the world. They'd fought the way siblings fought. They'd helped one another like siblings do. They had confided in each other as siblings do, about teenage crushes or the disappointments of adulthood. But Chaya never found anybody. She didn't let herself get involved. Her priorities have always been the Sarampião legacy and the park. And Thales understood this better than anyone. Which is why Chaya doesn't like where this conversation is going. She opens the door of the truck. Thales runs over and grabs hold of her.

"I'm sorry. I'm sorry. Don't leave." Thales hugs her. "I never think before speaking — isn't that what you always say? Forgive me, sis." Thales is still holding her.

"Enough with the melodrama, and enough talking shit, OK?"

"It's just . . . I'm desperate. I need your help."

"I'm not gonna talk to Enrico. You've always been scared of him, ever since you were a kid, you always had your mom as a go-between. Then she died and you tried to dump that responsibility on me. It's not gonna fly."

"It's not that I'm scared, I just don't know *how* to talk to him about Olga. He gets furious at just the sound of her name."

"Well, who doesn't round here? . . . Just grow up, Thales. You're the one who's got to do it."

"Are you going to be on my side?"

"You know what I think of Olga. She's not for you. You just can't see that . . ."

Chaya hears the rangers' radio beeping inside the truck. She picks up the handset:

"Chaya here. Over."

"*Officer Nestor here, Chaya. We need you in the park. Over.*"

"What's so urgent? Over."

"*India-01. Over.*"

"What's up?" asks Thales.

"Which side? Over," Chaya asks, still holding the radio.

"*Southwest. Over.*"

"Big?"

"*Definitely looks like it could get that way.*"

"Fucking hell, Nestor. We haven't had an India-01 in the park for years. Oh shit. Shit! I'm on my way. Over and out." She starts up the engine, turns on the headlamps.

A worried Thales asks her again:

"Talk to me. What's up?"

"Fire in the park. We need firemen, military police, civil police, the ICMBio team from Passo Fundo. Tell your dad and whoever else you can."

Red Alert

Olga is smoking a cigarette inside her car, parked in the deserted alley behind Chaya's place. The house, situated on a large plot of land, faces a main street, far busier with cars and people. Round back, where Olga's sitting, is the greenhouse built more than thirty years ago by Chaya's grandfather. From this vantage, Olga can follow any movement in the house. For now its lights are off, so she has turned her attention to every person, every car passing, waiting for any movement at all, any sign that Chaya might have arrived home. They hadn't agreed on a time. In the flurry of messages they had exchanged when Olga was on her way, Chaya had just said she'd be home tonight.

The black smartphone is on top of the dash. She takes the computer from her bag and opens it on her lap. The fingers of her left hand are holding her cigarette, and with her right, she types: "*Who is behind the Gran Roncador Binational hydroelectric project on the Brazil-Argentina border?"* Startled by the sound of sirens and cars approaching, she tosses the cigarette out of the window. She shuts the laptop and shrinks down in her seat. A fire truck rushes past, siren blaring. Then, trailing it, a series of cars with headlamps raised, and police cars, all headed in the same direction. She drops her laptop onto the passenger seat and gets out. Even from the side street, the lights of the police cars throw their colors onto her face.

Olga walks over to the corner and looks toward the horizon, to the right, where the cars are headed. In the distance she sees the unusual brightness of the flames that, at this moment, are spreading across the southwest edge of the Turvo park.

Trepeiros

It's after midnight. The blaze is consuming a whole chunk of the southwest section of the Turvo park. The Red Foot who were tasked with starting the fire have crossed the river by boat and returned to the Argentine side. All except León.

León runs through the forest, away from the flames. Every few moments, he turns to look back and sees the yellowish brightness in the distance. He smiles, proud. His tired legs ache, right up in his thighs, but he doesn't stop or slow his pace. Before dawn he will arrive at the place where Preta has set up camp.

Preta is sitting in a trepeiro: a wooden treestand. She's camouflaged, with the added cover of branches, leaves, and the total dark of the night. Her gun is pointed downward. Tied to one side of the tree there is bait of corn, leftovers of food and of raw meat. A pen made of bamboo and old wooden planks is a little further off. At the tops of three other trees close to Preta's, also on trepeiros, are two other women and one man, each holding a gun. All silent. Focused. They hear the hoarse pant of a creature approaching. The animal finds the bait on Preta's tree and begins to feed. A .44 rifle shot from the leader of the Red Foot hits the agouti in the back. It gives one short shrill cry, then falls to the side, dead.

"Open up its belly and dump the guts nearby. Leave the flesh down here. That'll bring the jaguar in."

Bone-Grinder

By four in the morning, hundreds of residents of Dourado are gathered in a soy field near the edge of the park, where the fire is progressively overtaking the forest. They're all talking at once, some are yelling, others crying. There are two fire trucks parked here. Firefighters and police officers are working together to try to contain the blaze. Local residents get dry earth in buckets and fling it onto the smaller fires, others are holding big branches, which they're using to beat down slightly larger ones. A third group, organized by Chaya's friend Dóris, a civil police officer, and by Thales, take bowls and even saucepans and fill them at a water-tank truck. There are even some who, in desperation, try to use the fire extinguishers from their own cars.

Standing beside one of the firefighters, Chaya helps hold the fire truck's hose. At the same time, she's calling out to the civilians around her:

"Be careful!"

Nothing seems to make any difference. The fire is growing. Two ladies start to pray:

"God help us! Our father who art in heaven . . ."

Birds shriek. Some fly out of the woods, but immediately drop to the ground, flailing. A family of coatis emerges from amid the flames. Their feet and fur are singed. A peccary appears next. It faints. Half its belly and its whole muzzle are burned. Other animals emerge, all wounded. The community tries to save them, but all are in a very bad way.

The tank on one of the fire trucks runs dry. Chaya looks around for some sort of salvation, a miracle. The man who had been helping her hold the hose gives up. The water's all done. After a brief hesitation, she drops it too and moves away. She sees people in torment. The burned animals, some dying, others dead. The firemen and the police officers look defeated. The fire ever taller, ever stronger. Everything seems to be happening in slow motion: people's gestures, their voices becoming slow, drawling. She feels a terrible shapeless pain, as if her bones are being ground. Chaya Sarampião, head of the Turvo park, cannot put out the fire that will destroy this conservation area for good, she thinks. The loud, deep rumble of a motor brings her back to reality. It's coming from above. She looks up and sees the lights of a twin-engine plane overhead. It opens its tanks, and the water falls onto the forest flames. Then another plane flies by. Chaya feels her legs give way. She kneels.

"Arrê."

People clap, they smile, they celebrate. Enrico comes over to Chaya and holds out his hand, but she doesn't take it, her eyes still fixed on those planes.

"You know, child, it wasn't easy, it was expensive and very risky what with it being the dead of night, but I managed to get them to come out as fast as possible."

Chaya turns to Enrico and finds a curious expression on his face, as if he were trying to conceal a sense of obligation, of duty. She gets up and hugs him.

"They'll do as many sorties as needed," he assures her, "whatever they've got to do to put the blaze out completely."

Chaya hangs from his neck without a word.

1997
Red Corcel

First One to Do It Wins

Chaya is in Enrico's study, beside a white wooden dollhouse with a whole elaborate setup inside it. She's holding a little pink plastic baby. Putting it down on the floor, she picks up a blond doll, with long smooth hair, blue eyes, and long lashes. She removes all its clothes. She looks at its legs, its arms, and its belly before giving a scream and hurling the toy at the glass of the bookcase. The noise of the impact is loud.

Enrico and Galliana, his wife, run in.

"What happened, child?" Galliana asks, but Chaya doesn't reply. Her sulky expression gets worse.

"When you scream like that, we think you've hurt yourself, Chaya. One day you really will get hurt and nobody will come to look after you," scolds Enrico.

Galliana throws her husband a reproachful look.

"What on earth happened?" he goes on.

"Don't you want to go outside and play with Thales and the other children?" His wife takes Chaya's little hands that are clenched, ready for a fight.

"Don't you like this house we gave you for your birthday? We can always give it to another child," says Enrico, and once again is rebuked by his wife.

"I don't like them," says Chaya, pointing at the doll she's thrown on the floor and the others inside the house.

"Why?"

"None of them look like me."

Enrico picks the blond doll up from the floor, along with the baby and all the others, and throws them into a drawer.

"Tomorrow the four of us will go into Porto Alegre to buy new toys," he says.

The expression on Chaya's face changes. She doesn't smile, but her eyes are shining. Enrico continues:

"Now let's go outside and sing you happy birthday, my child."

"I'm not your child." Chaya closes up again, folding her arms and leaning back against a wall. She will not be moved.

"Very well. You're right," says Galliana. "Enrico only said that because he meant we love you as if you were part of the family, *as if* you were our child. You do understand, don't you?"

Chaya starts to cry. Her crying begins very quietly and soon grows into a wail:

"I want my grandpa. Grandpa . . ."

Thales runs in and hugs Chaya.

"Why's she crying? What did you say to her?" He holds her.

Soon the girl begins to calm down, but her sobbing continues. "I'll stay here with you, sis." Thales wipes away the tears that are still streaming down her cheeks.

Enrico and Galliana watch the two children clinging to one another, protecting one another, like biological siblings. It is a love they have never witnessed before.

"Let's go out and talk to the guests. We don't need to sing happy birthday today. All right?" Enrico leads his wife out.

"Want to go to your room?" Thales asks.

"I wanna go to yours."

They hold hands and go to the bedroom. Chaya sits on the floor, Thales on the bed.

"Want to play?" he asks.

"Yeah."

Thales takes out a box of superhero figures.

"You didn't like your presents?" He hands her a Batman doll.

"No! I wanted a red Corcel like the one you've got." She points at the shelf with dozens of miniature cars.

"This one?" He picks out the red car with the black stripe painted on it.

"Yeah."

"This isn't a Ford Corcel."

"Is too. My grandpa Armin taught me all about cars. Totally everything."

The two of them laugh. Thales hands her the car.

"Have it, then. The Corcel is yours. My birthday present for you."

She holds the toy, fascinated. She plays with it for a few moments, then goes over to the box where her brother keeps his figurines and rummages around till she finds a blue one. Mystique from X-Men. She places her on top of the car and pretends they're flying.

"Let's go after the bad guys."

Thales picks out a convertible from the many remote control cars he has, he puts the Batman doll inside, turns on the motor, and sets it running about the bedroom floor.

"I'll stay on the ground, that way they can't get away, Mystique."

"Good thinking, Batman."

The two of them play until Thales's car goes under the bed and crashes into the wall.

"They got me! Help!"

The two children laugh.

"You know I'd be spending my birthday with my grandpa Armin if Preta hadn't killed him?"

"But didn't he have a hurt inside his head?"

"She's the one who did it."

"Right, yeah, like she totally has the superpower to put cancer into people's heads. That's how your grandpa died."

Chaya starts crying again, but just quietly this time.

"Sorry. I'm sorry. I was just kidding."

She sits back down on the floor and lets go of the Corcel.

"Want me to go steal some sweets for us to eat here?" he asks, and Chaya nods.

Thales walks over to the door, but before opening it he stops and says:

"I've had a great idea. Let's make this whole big obstacle course with like *all* the superheroes — we've got to go through it with your Corcel without knocking any of them over. First one to do it wins. OK?"

"OK." Chaya gets up, suddenly cheerful, and gives a little victorious leap.

"Start setting it up. I'll be right back, sis."

1958
The End

Armin and Roscato

Armin lowers the rowboat into the water, which is calm this afternoon, then slowly makes his way across the Uruguai. As he puts distance between himself and the Pari port, he feels the slight pull of current. On the Argentine side, he ties the craft to a tree and makes his way into the forest.

Half an hour later he arrives at the outcrop; the low vegetation and the boulders in particularly stark contrast because of the drought that's been going strong these past months, killing off what little grass once existed in this place. He hears barking in the distance, then a few voices. He approaches the four shacks in the middle of the forest. At the far side, there's a large wooden shed with a beaten earth floor. Three children burst out, two girls and a boy, all barefoot, wearing only shorts.

"Where are your parents?"

"Put your hands up and turn around slowly," a voice behind him gives the command.

Armin obeys. He is surprised to see Tédi pointing a shotgun at him. Beside her, a huge man, broad-shouldered, with a square jaw, thick eyebrows, is holding a machete. Before he can say a word, the man comes over and fells him with a blow from the machete's wooden handle.

Armin regains consciousness. It's pitch black around him, and silent. He feels the loose, dry earth finding its way into his mouth and his nostrils. He tries to get up but he's groggy. That blow to the head was fierce. He puts his hands behind his neck. There's something slick on his scalp. He sniffs it. It's blood. He feels around and finds a wooden wall. Supporting himself on it, he sits up. The minutes pass. The dark is absolute. Somebody opens the door and the brightness of the oil lamp blinds him.

"You're pretty brave," a voice says.

Armin's eyes gradually recover their sight, and he makes out the shape of a woman sitting down on a tree stump in front of him.

"Tédi, how about a bit of water, please?" Armin asks, still dizzy.

"What misfortune have you brought us now?"

"The two of you disappeared months ago, I haven't heard anything from you or Lenara since. How is the girl?"

"Better here than in that shithole you left us."

"I was trying to do what was best for her . . ."

His sister-in-law gets up and punches him in the eye. He falls down, and this time he just lies there. He hadn't expected the aggression, still less such strength.

"I owed you that. And how about Gringa? That bitch is gonna get what's coming to her."

awaiting them. Roscato watches an animal's life leave its eyes, and that brings him satisfaction. It feeds him, makes him feel bigger than he is, better. Armin doesn't have that same coldness, that thirst for killing. Even as the younger son, it fell to him to take care of and worry about their father and mother, and this sense of family is why he's here in this place, looking for his brother.

"Come on, brother, sit with me," Armin entreats him. "Sit and talk. For our dad. For your daughter. I'm asking you."

Roscato pulls his brother up from the floor and they stand face-to-face in silence. Something unspoken that is troubling.

"I killed Mad Mouth," says Roscato.

"What's that?"

"I killed him. I was with Caco on the hunt that day."

Armin launches himself at his brother and thumps him in the chest. The two men exchange blows, Roscato punching his brother in the stomach, making Armin back away.

"He paid me. Paid me to go with him. I was the only one who could kill that jaguar."

"You don't deserve the surname you have."

"I don't give a shit about this fucking name! A name that was made up by our coward of a great-grandfather we never even knew and who just showed up here at the border running away from a war. To hell with that surname. *Sarampião.* To hell with Mad Mouth, and Caco, and our father too . . ."

Armin is onto Roscato again, and the older brother suddenly finds himself on the defensive. Armin lands a punch on his nose, which breaks and starts to bleed.

"Enough! That's enough!" Roscato runs his hand over his blood-ied face, then starts to laugh, a laugh that is devilish.

"You're such a bastard," says Armin.

"Oh, that I am. A bastard. And I'm only telling you this because Tédi said I had to. You should live and die knowing that our dad . . ."

"Your time's up, Armin," Tédi interrupts them. "You can take him away."

Roscato moves as if he were drunk. A thick drool escapes his mouth, wetting his thin lips. He picks up the oil lamp in one of his hands and draws the gun from his waistband with the other.

"What about him — what about Dad? Did you see Dad that day?"

Roscato doesn't answer.

"Do you know where he is, Roscato? Tell me, please," Armin yells.

"Shut that trap of yours, Armin. There are kids sleeping," says Tédi. "Go, before I change my mind."

"Please," Armin begs his brother, "talk to me."

The man with the thick eyebrows reappears. He takes Armin by both arms and shoves him out.

"Better be the last time I see you this side of the river, Armin. My rules are gonna be enforced if you find yourself on our turf again," says Tédi.

Armin, Roscato, and the other man walk past the rocky outcrop, through the woods, and arrive at the riverbank. The man puts Armin into the small boat. He unties it from the tree. Roscato is right behind them. He hands his brother the lamp. They push the boat off. Armin is trembling all over. His face is frozen in shock.

"Roscato! Is Dad alive? Is Dad still alive, brother?"

Roscato disappears into the forest, with the other man following behind.

A Pact of Silence

First thing the next morning, Armin arrives at Gringa's grocery store. Enrico is kneeling on the wooden stool, behind the counter. He takes some money out of a drawer, counts it, and jots down sums in a notebook.

"Hey, kid, tell your mom I'm here, please," says Armin.

"Morning," Enrico says but he doesn't move.

Armin vaults over the counter and goes through the curtain that leads to the back of the store. Enrico runs to try to grab him, but Armin shoves him away. He marches down the corridor till he spots Gringa. She's sweaty, red-faced, lugging a heavy sack of cornflower from a pile to the back door, where there's a truck parked. Two employees, both young men, watch her.

"You get it? If I can do it, these two princesses here can too." She spots Armin, followed closely by a furious Enrico.

"Go out front, take care of the business, son," Gringa tells him, then she turns to Armin. "Let's go into the house, my friend. Time for us to have that chat."

In the living room of the Romanos' house, Armin is standing close to the door. Gringa is in an armchair, under the large living-room window. She gives a hoarse cough, clearing her throat into a handkerchief. Armin looks outside. His eyes are burning, a burning from the dryness of the day and the low humidity in the air, mixed with the certainty that what he used to think of as a family misfortune was now transforming into something much worse. A curse befalling the Sarampião and Romano families.

"This conversation never leaves this room," says Armin. "Never. Now you do whatever you have to but I don't want to know any details." He wants to conclude the conversation and get out as fast as possible.

"And then we shut this subject down for good, right, Armin? For those who are left in our family, the best thing we can do is not tell anybody and get on with our lives. And whatever you, Idalina, and Amara need, you can count on me," says Gringa.

"We're done now. I'm leaving for Dourado. I know we're both losing a lot, but I can't keep running into you every day, pretending I don't know what happened and nor can you. Keep away from my family and I'll keep away from yours. Bye, Gringa."

Gringa watches Armin leave. They both know this isn't the end of the pain caused by those tragedies that have befallen them, tragedies that will never be forgotten.

Armin leaves through the front yard, crosses the gravel plot of the grocery store, and arrives on the street. He dodges a family of three whom he knows, and who, as he passes, try but fail to greet him. He climbs onto the cart that's stopped on the berm of the road.

"Let's go, Zebruno. Let's go, Branco." He goads the oxen on, hard, and the wagon starts up. The red dried-earth road throws up a thick cloud of dust, covering not just him but also what is now past and to be concealed, but will never be forgotten.

Neither Heaven nor Hell

Two months later, Lenara, looking older than her thirteen years, wears a black dress that comes down to just above her knees, and leather lace-ups. She's a tall thin girl, having grown a lot in the past year, with broad shoulders, her long hair loose. Her mother, Tédi, by contrast, has short blond hair streaked with gray, and wears snug blue sweatpants that emphasize the muscles in her thick legs, a white tank top, and a golden chain level with her breasts. At her waist she carries a .38 caliber revolver. They're holding hands by an open grave at the back of the cemetery, in the old part of the village, in the rural part of Corredera Moconá. Inside it, a coffin made of old planks of wood and a cross, on which is written: *Roscato Sarampião — b. 1927 — d. 1958.*

Tédi takes out a small bottle of cachaça. She opens it and pours a small amount onto the coffin; finally she drops the bottle into the grave. Lenara just watches, smelling the strong liquor mingling with the freshly dug earth.

"One day Armin's gonna pay. . . . They all will," says Tédi.

Armin, Idalina, and their daughter, Amara, are inside the Turvo woods, close to the Yucumã Falls. Each holds a candle.

"You should have gone to the funeral," Idalina says loudly, intending to be heard over the thunderous roar of the waterfall.

Armin doesn't reply. He just looks at his hands linked around the candle, his thumbs brushing against each other, showing his impatience.

"Tédi thinks it was you who turned Roscato over to the police. Your absence at his funeral will only give her more reason."

Armin stays silent. Rage courses through him, but he doesn't show it. He is resolved: he will never again speak his brother's name nor talk about that night he crossed the river to find him, let alone about what happened next. The shameful memory of Roscato is his cross to bear. One day it will disappear, as if he'd simply never existed.

"I'm gonna light my candle for Uncle Roscato," says Amara.

Armin grips the girl's wrist. She gives a little cry. He shouts louder:

"No!" And then the tone of his voice changes, trying to seem calm. "No — these candles are for your grandpa Sarampião."

"But it was grandpa Sarampião who asked me to light mine for my uncle," Amara says, alarmed by her father's reaction.

"How can this girl be talking this sort of nonsense now? It's not right to make up stories, child, specially not with your grandpa's name."

Upset, Amara runs off toward a cabralea and hides behind its trunk. Armin makes as if to go after her, but Idalina stops him.

Gringa and Enrico are at the grocery store. Four people are waiting their turn while Gringa gives a can of pork lard to a woman and Enrico passes over her change. Before leaving, the woman places her hand on Gringa's and says:

"Divine justice has been done for Caco, Dona Romano. Just knowing that layabout Roscato hanged himself in prison has left a lot of people here in town feeling very relieved."

Gringa grabs the woman's arm, sticking her nails into the flesh.

"What's divine justice got to do with this? Can you tell me that? You're no better than a parasite, feeding on other people's misfortune. Get the hell out my sight. You're not buying from here again."

The store owner's reaction catches the woman by surprise. She staggers a few steps back then hurries out. Enrico watches his red-faced mother, as she starts to cough. She takes a handkerchief out of her shirt pocket and spits. Her eyes come to rest, silently, on the blood mixed with catarrh at the bottom of the piece of cloth.

Blood

Keep Your Enemy Close

It's October 31, and the sun is already up. A tall dark plume of smoke continues to rise out of the forest. The powerful stench of burning still hangs in the air. Dozens of people remain around the southwestern part of the park. There are small patches of fire yet to be put out, and the military brigade are working on them with the help of volunteers. The fire trucks head back to their station in town. Chaya's face, arms, and legs are covered in ash and earth. She is engrossed, staring at the red-hot trunks and branches of whatever trees are still standing in the area. Cláudio appears, clean-faced, his hair wet and neatly combed, in an ironed ranger's uniform, and he holds out a bottle of water.

"Hey, boss."

She takes the bottle. She tries to smile, but nothing comes.

"You ought to go home, get some rest," he says.

Chaya feels the weight of that word — *boss.*

He goes on:

"I've showered, had a rest — I can stay here through the morning, or all day. If you'd like me to, of course."

She drinks some of the water, then throws what's left over her hands and face.

"You're right. I've got to pull myself together. You stay here, Cláudio, you can guide the biologist and the vets who're arriving soon. Anything you don't know, radio through to HQ or get them to call me."

"You've done a great job," Cláudio says.

"Have you guys tracked the collars on the jaguars and the puma?"

"Yes, boss. Two of the jaguars are still on the Argentine side. The puma and the other jaguar shifted location early in the morning to the opposite side of the park."

"Arrê!" She takes a deep breath. "When we manage to get back in, we'll be able to know how many animals we've lost, and which ones."

Cláudio says sadly:

"I think our cameras are gone."

Chaya gently touches her colleague's shoulder then walks slowly to the truck. She's surprised to see Thales and Dóris sitting on the pickup's wooden tailgate. The two of them are as dirty and exhausted as she is.

"You're still here?"

"We're not leaving till you do," Thales says.

"And I just bet him a six-pack that's going to be right now," says Dóris, smiling.

"We're gonna drink that beer together."

Chaya knocks on the window of Olga's car, startling her awake. She rolls down the window.

"Don't tell me you spent the night here."

"I had nowhere else to go." Olga opens the door and gets out. "You didn't answer my calls."

"It was a hellish night. Literally. Get your things and let's go inside."

"That smoke is really bad out here," Olga says, wrinkling her nose at the stench. "Was it very rough?" she asks, picking up her laptop and purse.

"Watching a forest burn is never fun." Chaya opens the back gate and walks toward her house.

Olga goes round to fetch her suitcases from the trunk. She briefly thinks to ask Chaya for help, she does have two heavy bags, but quickly drops the idea when she registers her former classmate's filthiness and exhaustion. They walk through the gate, across the yard, past grandpa Armin's famous greenhouse. Entering the house through the kitchen, Olga sets her suitcase, her laptop, and her purse down before walking into the living room where Chaya is waiting. Chaya points at the four-seater sofa.

"You can rest there. Turn on the TV if you want, grab a book to read," Chaya gestures toward the crammed bookcase over to one side of the room. "I need a bath and a few hours' sleep. I'm not thinking straight right now."

"Go. Sleep. I've got a lot to show you. I need you to be switched on."

Chaya disappears down the corridor that leads to the bedroom. But then she calls back:

"And no smoking inside. And if anyone knocks, wake me first, don't open the door."

It's past midday when Chaya rises. She gets dressed and walks over to the kitchen. Olga has prepared some coffee and made scrambled eggs and fried steak, and set the table with bread and cream, jam and a jar of cookies.

"It was the least I could do for you," Olga says with an embarrassed smile.

"For me? Oh, no. You did it for yourself, Olga. Like everything else." Chaya sits down, puts a piece of meat on her plate, cuts off a bit, and begins to chew. "It's done just right. I can say that much, at least."

"So polite, as usual. Eat up, cause after you've seen what I'm going to show you, you won't have much of an appetite."

The two women are standing over the dining table in the living room. On a glass countertop, up against one of the walls, there are picture frames displaying old photos of Sarampião, of Chaya's grandfather, Armin, with her grandmother, Idalina, and also her mother, Amara, pregnant.

"Your mom?" Olga picks up the photo.

"Yeah."

"You never told me what happened to her."

"What the fuck, Olga — are we supposed to be best friends now?" Chaya looks at the pieces of paper laid out over the table. "Any chance this is some setup, a trap?"

"This here, it's the log from the phone carrier, the date, the codes. It's real. This whole heap of calls to his number. Not to mention sums with Enrico's name written next to them. There's no doubt at all." Olga is categorical.

"How could I have been so blind?" Chaya feels a weight in her chest. She tries to disguise it, but her lips are turning pale. Olga notices.

"Want to take a break? We can look at the rest later."

"I've got to think." Chaya looks at Olga. "You could have put all this together just because you wanted to get back at Enrico."

"I know it must be hard for you, but I've got the contracts, the documents, account numbers, records of deposits to prove it. I'm really sorry, Chaya. I know he was a father to you, he was your family for . . ."

"Just shut it, you hear me? You don't know a damn thing." Chaya shoves the papers away.

"Whoa, you're angry with *me*? For bringing evidence, for telling the truth and opening your eyes? Instead of with Enrico? That bastard . . ."

"See what I mean? Everything for yourself. You hate him."

"I'm doing it because I promised I'd help you find out who in Dourado was involved with Gran Roncador. I'm doing it because these people can't keep getting away with everything."

There are so very many thoughts, memories, conversations with Enrico running through Chaya's head. She's dizzy. She pulls up a chair and sits down. Guilty people lie, they pretend with an unquestionable truthfulness. He's fooled everyone. She regrets having allowed herself to stay in that bubble of security and common interest, in which she thought she lived, in which everyone in that town thought they lived. She betrayed her instinct when she began to grow suspicious of Enrico and did nothing about it.

"And Thales . . ." says Chaya.

"No, he's not mixed up in this. He's the opposite of your dad—you know that better than anyone."

"Of course I do. But I also know he loves and idolizes Enrico.

Listen to me: Thales can't know about any of this. He's got a big mouth, he could spill the beans even if he doesn't mean to," Chaya warns her, then gets to her feet. "I'm serious, Olga. We've got to be rational now." She takes her phone from her pants pocket and starts to photograph the documents.

"Did Thales tell you?"

"Look, Olga, we haven't suddenly become confidantes, you and me, OK? I'm not here to chat about your love life, especially if it's got anything to do with Thales."

"You really don't think enough time has passed? That you might try to forgive me?"

"And have you ever asked for my forgiveness?"

"Well, I'm here now . . ."

"Enough chat. We've got to deal with Enrico, with Heichma and this power plant. But nothing else."

"Will you be able to lie to him?"

"What do you mean?"

"He's your brother. Clearly you care what he'd think, how he'll react."

"I'm not going to lie. I'll leave some details out, and I'll do that out of love. You're right, Thales is the only person alive I care about, and I'll do whatever I can to protect him. And that's why it's better to keep him in the dark. It's also why I think he deserves someone better than you. Just 'cause you've brought me all this doesn't mean you've changed."

Olga gets up, leaves the dining room, goes to the kitchen, gets some water, drinks. She looks out of the window at Armin's greenhouse. She thinks about the teenager she was back then, about the mistakes she made, the regrets she carries with her. Her hand trembles. She has had to bear too mch. No more concessions. She goes back to Chaya.

“Look, I know I've been an asshol know you have every reason not to believe I'm doing things diffently now, trying to be a different person. But I also know that th isn't the only truth about me that exists. There's another one, anm gonna find it. Which is why I asked your help in tracking him dn . . .”

“That again.”

“I need to find Sarampião.”

“Oh man, just because you're in house, don't think I won't beat the crap out of you . . .”

“I told you I'd bring all the ence, and I only asked for one thing,” Olga insists. “Just one thin

“After what you did? Don't youe any shame at all?”

Olga's confused, she doesn'ow what to reply. But Chaya goes on:

“You disrespected, scorned mmily's memory, doing what you did in that square. You diminishhe importance of Sarampião to this town, to me. You mocked tanctity of a place that's sacred to all those who loved SarampiAnd before that, you even tried to make a fool of me in the claoom, at school. What for, Olga? What for?”

“I was wrong. I was blind, I watrying to get revenge. You tried to break me and Thales up severa times, till you finally managed it. You were always a dick for no reason. I'd had it up to here that day, Chaya. I was no saint, but you . . . This conversation won't get us anywhere.”

“It really won't. Forget about Sarampião.”

Olga starts to gather the papers back up from the table.

"I'm not going to Argentia, I'm not going to finish writing the exposé for any newspaper. None of this means anything if I can't at least try to ask Sarampião's forgiveness. It's either that or I dump all this crap in the Uruguai."

"Stop," says Chaya. "You're pain in the ass, Olga, you know that? OK. But you have no idea wh you're in for."

"I'll manage."

"Well, get ready: it's gon have to be tonight. You can't stay in Dourado any longer." She ru her fingers over her eyes, then over her eyebrows. Olga smiles. ya notices, which gets her even angrier. "Put those teeth awa eed you to send me all the photos you took in that office, th ording of your conversation with Heichma, the documents o memory stick. I'll put everything for safekeeping in multiple s."

"I've got it in mine alread

"And what if they catch What if they kill you? We need to save it in other places, for in ce."

Once again, Olga has tha e feeling she had the day before, when she was collecting the uments from the office, only now multiplied manyfold. Her legs her chin are trembling. She looks for a chair and sits. Chaya seen that expression before. She understands what it's like to e a volcano erupting within your body. *Olga cannot give up now,* haya thinks.

"Olga, look at me. Look into y eyes. Easy now. Breathe through your mouth. That's it. Let's coun to ten together."

They count. Olga takes Chaya's hands. Chaya tries to free herself but ends up letting her hold them. Olga begins to calm down. Chaya keeps talking:

"You said it yourself, you're doing the right thing. Only one side of this will make history and be remembered forever, and it's not theirs, it's the side of the journalist who's going to expose these people. You'll be safe in Argentina. Keep writing that article. Don't let yourself be intimidated. You're not weak. You're not fearful. If there's something you're not and never have been, it's that. You know, I envied you that when we were at school."

"I never thought I'd hear that from you."

"Well, it's true."

"Thank you."

Chaya heads for the front door. Before leaving, she says:

"You're sure they'll publish it in that paper? That they won't leak anything beforehand? You really trust them?"

"It's our best chance. Yeah, I do trust them . . . I have to."

Every War Is a Deal

That same day Heichma and Senna are standing in the underground garage of the Rio Grande do Sul Legislative Assembly, next to a black car. The driver's door is open. Senna tosses the rest of his cigarette on the ground and crushes it with his shoe.

"They haven't managed to locate her cell phone?" asks Heichma.

Senna shakes his head. He's nervous.

"We don't know what she has," he says. "But I can't exactly imagine she'd go to the Public Prosecutor's. She doesn't have the courage for that — or even the intelligence. I mean, who'd take her seriously?"

"Jesus fucking Christ, Senna," Heichma mutters in Senna's ear, "she already had the guts to do what she did, clearly she's going to try to show it to people. What's in your notebook and my safe alone would be enough to screw everything up. For now, no one in Brasília can know."

against the wall, between a cupboard and the fridge, under the window. Footsteps circle the house, then two men's voices.

"Looks empty," says one.

"Yeah, all quiet. Shall we go round the back?"

From Olga's position, she catches the shadows of the men reflected in the glass of the crockery cabinet in front of her as they stop at the window. Her heart races. One of them tries to force the back door. Once, twice, three times. Olga realizes she has forgotten her phone on the table.

"Shall we smash the window?" asks the second man.

"You're the boss."

Still hugging her computer, Olga crawls toward the laundry area. The men break the glass. Olga shudders and hides under the big sink.

A car pulls up in the backyard. The men are scared, and Olga hears hurried footsteps, followed by a third voice yelling:

"Next time I'm calling the police, assholes."

Olga recognizes that voice—it's Thales. A moment later, she hears him talking, leaving a voicemail:

"Chaya, where are you? Call me, it's urgent. Ricci and some other weird guy were here in your yard. They said they'd arranged to meet you but one of your windowpanes was smashed in. I nearly called the police."

Olga rushes over and opens the door. Thales is surprised to see her. She hugs him, saying:

"Thanks."

The sun is beginning to set. The pickup turns the corner at full speed, before coming to an abrupt stop on the sidewalk in front of

Chaya's house. Chaya throws the car door open, pulls her gun from its holster, and gripping it tight, steps onto her property, walking around the exterior of the house before slowly opening the kitchen door. She finds Olga and Thales sitting at the table drinking coffee.

"Hey, Chaya — take it easy. You can put the gun away," says Thales.

She does so.

"Did they see you, Olga?" she asks.

"No, I hid under the laundry sink."

Chaya notices the broken windowpane.

"Was that them?"

Olga nods.

"I'll take Olga to Argentina," says Thales. "It's safer."

"Did you tell him?"

"That I'm going to Argentina." Olga raises an index finger, hoping to warn Chaya not to say any more.

"Thales, best you keep out of it. Thanks for letting me know — but you can go now."

"Why are you being so rude?" he asks.

"I'm not being rude. . . . Yeah, OK. Sorry. You know I'm overwhelmed with problems out in the park. But I don't need your help. Go back to the hotel."

"Chaya's right," says Olga. "You should go."

"I don't recognize you two right now. Are you going to explain what's happening? Are you going to explain this sudden alliance?"

"There's nothing happening," says Chaya, "and there is absolutely *no* alliance."

"Look, those guys weren't messing about. I'm not leaving my sister and my . . . and Olga here alone."

Chaya starts to laugh. She takes the gun and puts it on the table.

"I think we can manage without you, bro."

"You've been a lot of help already," says Olga.

"Thales, I need you to promise you won't tell anyone you saw Olga here. Not even your dad."

"Dad? Why would he do anything to Olga. Come on, sis, there's something weird going on. Tell me."

"You do trust me, don't you? Well then, it's better for nobody in town to know Olga's here. She's about to leave anyway, and then everything will be fine." Chaya takes Thales's hand and leads him to the door.

"If you say . . ." Before leaving, Thales looks over at Olga. Chaya realizes this might be the last time in their lives they'll see one another. She swallows all her pride and allows her love for her adoptive brother to gain the upper hand. Without thinking too much about the consequences, she says:

"If you're just gonna stand there like a post, I'm going outside to park the truck properly and then call Maurício Ricci. To try to find out what the little rat was after. When I get back to this kitchen, I hope I won't find you still here," she says and squeezes Thales's hand, then she gives him a kiss on the cheek and leaves.

Olga and Thales don't move.

"Will you call me, or at least message me with news?" he asks her.

"Best we don't talk for a while."

Thales can't hide his despair. Olga goes on:

"But you never know, when I come back, maybe we can find our way back onto the same road again."

She steps forward and hugs him. A long hug. They kiss. Thales presses Olga's body to his. She tries to get away, but he won't let go.

"The two of us need to start again, as different people. This Olga and this Thales aren't good for one another," she says.

"And who's to say for sure that we'll be different people in future?"

"Nobody. But I'm gonna try." Olga pulls herself free from Thales's arms and steps away.

"If you take too long to find this new Olga, I'm coming after you, wherever you are."

Olga is broken. She can't imagine how much Thales will hate her after she lands his father in jail.

That Gray Look

Thales arrives back at the hotel. He strides quickly along the hallway and stops outside his father's study. He goes inside. There's no one there. He sits in the chair and tries to open the desk drawers, but they're locked. He feels around underneath for the key. His father appears. Thales jumps to his feet, not hiding his shock. He sees his father's gray eyes, and a heavier demeanor than usual.

"Did I startle you?"

"No. I was just looking for an estimate. You know the one. For the tiles in the bathrooms in the east wing." He tries to deflect.

"You heard anything from Olga?"

Thales looks at his father with some disappointment. A disappointment that soon turns to sadness. He shakes his head and moves away. Enrico notices that there's something up with his son.

"Thales, it's high time you listened to me about that girl. It's for your own good. You know if she's here in town?"

"How would I know?"

"Look, son, apparently she stole some things from Heichma's office and disappeared. Important things. Money, even. Seriously, the little slut better not be coming round here bringing more problems for you or for me." He takes a key from his shirt pocket and opens one of the desk drawers.

Thales watches him, and asks:

"It's strange, don't you think, father?"

"What's strange?"

"That they're involving you. In something to do[illegible]h the deputy's office."

"I know what I'm doing."

"Why not just have a few bottles of wine sent o[illegible]huh? Isn't that how you usually placate him?"

And Thales walks out.

Time Passes Faster When You Have No Time

It's a hot night, unusual for late October. Chaya forges ahead, her flashlight illuminating the trail through the Turvo forest. They are in the north, the opposite end to where the fire happened, but even at this distance, the smell of smoke still hangs in the air. Olga follows her in silence. In the fifty minutes they've been walking they haven't exchanged a word. Sweaty and tired, they feel better when they finally hear, albeit still quietly, the sound of the falls in the distance. When at last they arrive at the outcrop with a lot of stones and not much vegetation, Chaya takes an old blanket from her backpack and throws it down over a grassy patch.

"This is the place," she says.

"OK. I'll sit and wait. I have the flashlight on my phone."

"You're sure about this?"

"Yeah."

"We got more than forty thousand acres in the park; if you run, if you leave this spot, you'll get lost. Understand?"

"Where would I run to in this darkness?"

"They'll be the longest hours of your life, Olga."

"I can take it."

"I'll be back at dawn."

"I'll be here."

Without another word, Chaya walks away.

The darkness is absolute. Olga turns on her phone's flashlight with the calm of somebody who has not one but two portable chargers in her backpack, despite Chaya telling her, brusquely, that flashlights wouldn't be any use in that place. Sitting on the blanket, she arranges the backpack to serve as a pillow and lies down. She looks at the sky. She's never seen such a starry night. She remains in that state of contemplation, with that unprecedented sense of freedom, for ten, fifteen minutes. The feeling that, at this moment, her existence is somehow suspended in the air — until a mosquito bites her, and she slaps her cheek lightly, then takes the repellent out of her bag and spreads it over her skin. She hears a branch snap. Her heart jumps. She turns the weak light toward the sound, but sees nothing. An owl shrieks at the top of a tree. She looks for it, but can't see that either. A cricket chirps to her right, then a cicada. And then she hears the sound of footsteps. She can't tell exactly where they're coming from. She aims the beam of light in every direction.

"Who's there? I'm armed!"

She hears the same sound again. Closer this time.

"Sarampião?" she calls out. "Sarampião?"

A figure, a shape standing in front of her, not far away. She strains her eyes, but can't make out what it is. The shape moves. First it

The Paths That Lead to Hell

The first of November, a calm morning in Red Foot territory. In the center of the settlement two women, one young and the other old, are heating up water in aluminum kettles hanging from an iron bar over a fire. To one side, a pan of cassava is also cooking. Women and men come out of their homes, approach the hot water hanging from its ramshackle bridge, and wash their faces in it. Children and adolescents start to appear in the doorways and windows, swollen faces betraying their recent waking. The morning dew hangs on the grass, the bushes, and the few flowers around them.

Preta appears in the distance. She's walking slowly. Her demeanor is heavy. She's filthy, with earth and blood smeared all over her body and her clothes. A woman from the group breaks into a smile.

"She's back! La Jefa is back," she exclaims.

Behind Preta comes one woman from the hunt, followed by another two. They're carrying a pitanga tree trunk; tied to it, by the feet, is a dead jaguar. It's the Old Lady, as she was known. León and another two men from the hunt are further back, carrying a heavy Styrofoam cooler. Everybody looks exhausted and sad, all except for León, who makes no effort to hide a delight that makes the others uncomfortable.

The Red Foot stare at the dead Old Lady. Some of them put their hands over their mouths. Others even take a step back as the hunters approach with the jaguar. They drop the body on the ground, in front of the green house where Preta lives. Then they sit down beside the animal. Preta registers the sense of concern and distress in the air. She takes the lead:

"OK — so everyone pay attention to what we need to do now." She holds her voice firm. "Stay strong. You understand? Go fetch the larger planks and the trestles. Set up the table here. Put some more water to boil." She exhales, then swallows down thick acidic saliva. "Start skinning her and taking out the bones . . ." By the time Preta ends her speech, her voice is quiet, broken.

For a moment she looks down at the red earth, at her bare feet, tender and dirty. León approaches. He puts his hand on her arm, bringing her back to that place, to that moment, to her people.

"I can keep the tooth? Por favor?" he asks.

Preta looks at him. His face is turned toward the jaguar, his pupils are dilated, fixed on the dead creature's mouth. Preta's thoughts go immediately to her grandmother Tédi; then, without wishing it, to her great-grandfather Sarampião. She knows what that means. She knows what she needs to do. What should have been done already. But she isn't in the mood to talk to the boy. Not just now. She brushes off his hand, and as she walks away, she says:

"Keep it."

The jaguar's pelt has been stripped off, and it's stretched out over the branches of a tree. On the table set up in the middle of the Red Foot settlement, the animal's blood drains out and mixes with the grass and the dry earth. People are cutting up hunks of meat, which they put into thick plastic bags and throw into a huge grimy cooler. The bones are separated into another container. Likewise the other canine and the rest of the teeth. Everything will be sold.

León is sitting on the wooden step that leads to the green house where he lives with Preta. He is holding the Old Lady's canine happily. He uses a penknife to clean off the residue of cartilage, skin, and blood that still stick to it. Preta, who has just had her bath, her hair wet and loose, in clean clothes, sits down next to him. She still has the plaster tied around one of her legs, covering her wound.

"How do you feel?"

"Un hombre," he says.

"A man," she corrects him. "You have to stop speaking that Spanish. Talk like the Brazilians, so you can negotiate with them." Preta slaps the boy's ear lightly.

León pays her no attention. He continues with his cleaning.

"With every animal you kill, you become more of an animal, not more of a man." Preta elbows him in the belly, and he groans. "Never forget that."

A dog wanders over to the cooler containing the jaguar meat, sticks its muzzle inside and snaps up a bag. Before he's able to run off with it, León throws his penknife and manages to hit the animal's thigh, and it cries out. A shriek followed by yelping. The blade is stuck into the dog's leg, and it flees, limping, into the scrubland, leaving the bag of meat behind.

"Now finish what you started," Preta orders him.

"What?"

Preta goes into the house, and returns with an old .32 caliber revolver.

"Let's go!" she says.

León is frozen, looking at the gun in Preta's hand.

"Let's go!" Impatiently, Preta gives the command one last time and walks toward the woods. León follows her.

An Unanswered Prayer

Early in the afternoon, Heichma and Senna drive through the gateway into the town of Dourado. The thermometer on the clock in the square is showing thirty-eight degrees Celsius. The deputy slows the car and parks. The two men get out, walk to the fountain and the statue of Sarampião. Heichma points at a small chapel at the end of the road.

"Let's go in."

The two men enter. Only Heichma kneels. The politician's shirt is clinging to his body with sweat. He prays an Our Father. Senna is silent. Then they return to the car.

"You don't pray, Senna?"

"Honestly, deputy, something tells me praying ain't gonna help us with this one."

Heichma furrows his greasy brow. He crosses himself.

"Heavens! A man without God is empty inside."

Back in the car, they head to Romano's hotel and stop outside. Heichma alights and, aware of the impact of his presence here, loiters on the sidewalk outside the hotel shaking hands with passers-by. Some are happy to come over and greet him, others avoid him or even refuse to hold out their hands to his. But he is unfazed.

"I'm your deputy. I'm the one who brings money to this town," he declares loudly.

Enrico appears at the hotel entrance.

"Deputy? I didn't know you were in town, senhor."

"I needed to show up in person, Romano." Heichma is speaking sternly.

"You're not taking our calls, Romano." Senna claps Enrico sharply on the shoulder.

The politician greets a young couple who seem not altogether sure who he is, then goes over to join the two men.

"Come in," says Enrico. "Let's go out back to my office."

They walk the long hallway and enter the office. Enrico shuts the door. He sits at the desk, and with a wave of his hand, invites the others to settle into the two armchairs opposite.

"We want to talk to that Brazilian girl, that cabocla who's in charge of that bunch of outlaws across the border," begins Senna.

Heichma fiddles with his cell phone, pretends he's not paying attention.

"So, Heichma," says Enrico, "you've outsourced this important conversation to some assistant, then?"

"His chief of staff!" Senna snaps.

"I'm not here, I don't know anything about this conversation you're having." Heichma takes a newspaper from off the desk and pretends to read.

"We've learned from some neighbors that Olga's parents have gone to Argentina, to the province just across from here — Misiones. We believe Olga must be there too. So we want to talk to the cabocla. She's got power over there. Don't the Red Foot work for hire? For *la plata*, like they say over there? Well, we've got *plata*. . . ." says Senna.

"Preta isn't in charge of the whole region," Enrico explains, "only this bit near the border. She's a local leader — there are others further inland."

"Oh, don't think you can talk us into changing our minds, old man," says Senna. "We know how much she's feared, and she has more sway than anyone else. So figure out some way to get her out here to talk to us."

"It's obvious you have no understanding of a place like this, nor of groups like the Red Foot. If you want to talk to any man in charge in a place like that, to a woman in charge, you go to her."

Heichma gets up. He tosses the newspaper onto the chair where he'd been sitting and says:

"The two of you are going to cross the river tomorrow morning."

"No, deputy, hang on a sec . . ." Senna doesn't make it to the end of his sentence.

"You're very much to blame for this too," Heichma says loudly to his chief of staff, before addressing Enrico. "Try to arrange a meeting for tomorrow, Romano. Your life depends on it, man. Otherwise you'll be first on the chopping block. We need to get our hands on what Olga's got and destroy it."

Senna is downcast, a look of suffering on his face. Enrico puts one of his hands to his belly and makes no effort to hide his pained expression. Heichma walks over to the door and says before leaving:

"Have them sort out a nice room for me to spend the night. And you, Senna — get your shit together, because if anything goes wrong, I promise I will skin you alive. We don't leave till all this crap has been resolved."

Thales appears. He and Heichma cross paths.

"Afternoon," Heichma greets him. Thales doesn't reply.

Senna walks past him too. Thales waits a few moments, until the two men have disappeared down the hall, then he closes the office door.

"What do they want, Dad? What's going on?"

Enrico is apprehensive.

"Look, son, I've told you a thousand times: Don't get involved. Trust me. Best for you not to know anything."

Argentine Soil

That afternoon, Olga crosses the Uruguai River in a wooden motorboat, not a very large one. The sun is blazing. It is phenomenally hot. An Argentine man in a tank top and cap is steering the boat. In front of Olga, a small suitcase she has brought with her; on her lap, her backpack with her computer, her phone, and the documents. She looks all around her, in every direction, checks that no one is following her, even despite Chaya and the boatman assuring her, more than once, that in this bit of the park, through which she is making her clandestine departure, there wouldn't be a living soul around.

They arrive on Argentine soil. The boatman picks up the suitcase in one hand and a machete in the other. Olga puts on her backpack and follows him in. Gripping on to tree roots and trunks, they scale a steep and inaccessible bank, slick with mud. They reach a piece of forest that is dense but on more level ground. They will proceed in that direction. The man goes ahead, opens up their way with his blade. They walk about thirty minutes through the forest. Olga's arms and legs are scratched. It was a mistake to come in shorts, she thinks.

They hear a barking, then somebody's voice ordering their dog to be quiet. The Argentine stops them in their tracks, and they exchange a glance that is an agreement to stay silent. Slowly, he puts down the suitcase and, like somebody who was born in the heart of this place, he plunges in and disappears. Olga doesn't know what to do, so she hides behind the trunk of a tall apuleia and holds her breath. She takes off her backpack and hugs it. Alert to everything, she hears the cry of a harpy eagle. The sound comes from up above. She looks up and locates the bird sitting on a branch. Captivated by the white and gray feathers on its chest and wings, the iconic plumage of this species that's usually so hard to find, she ends up being distracted, so much so that she relaxes a little and sits down on the ground. A hand covers her mouth and nose. She tries to scream but cannot. She blinks once, twice. She sees her guide in front of her, and he puts his index finger over his lips asking her not to make a sound. He whispers to her in his local Portuñol:

"They cerca, very near."

In the back seat of a 1992 Ford Falcon coupe that is so old and rickety that it's actually missing a passenger door, Olga smokes a cigarette as she stares out at the intense green of the landscape. The driver sports aviators and a beer belly. The boatman is in the passenger seat, his right arm holding on to the safety strap. He seems unperturbed to be riding in a car without a door.

They arrive at a village on the edge of Corredera Moconá, in

Misiones province. They stop outside a small building with a façade painted light blue and white and, in the center, the Argentine flag. The bars protecting the building's wooden doors and windows are rusty old iron, with leftover flakes of paint suggesting a time when it was all painted brown. On the third floor, it's possible to make out the orange curtains behind the dusty windowpanes. Over the small entrance, there's a sign written in gold letters: HOTEL.

Olga gets out of the car through the side that has no door. The Argentine pops the trunk and hands over her luggage. He says nothing. It's Olga who speaks:

"Gracias."

He nods and returns to the car. The two men leave. Olga looks out over that inhospitable landscape. Inhospitable at least to her reality. She can't make out what is right and what is wrong in this new life she has just entered. *How has all this, this whole change of worlds, happened so fast?* she asks herself.

She walks into her room at the hotel and switches on the light. She turns the key twice, then takes a chair and wedges it up against the latch. The walls are time-stained white, there's a double bed with an orange bedspread to match the drapery, and a minuscule bathroom. Off to one side she sees a small table and chrome metal chair with visible patches of rust, the sofa opposite the ancient TV set, with a built-in antenna attached, and the minibar, empty and turned off, next to the bed, serving as a nightstand. She puts down her backpack, takes out her computer and switches it on. She tests the wi-fi. It works fine, actually. She sighs with relief. A good feeling that she's experiencing for the first time that afternoon since she said goodbye to Chaya on the riverbank. She opens the curtain a little to let some of the fading daylight into the room. She takes her cell phone, checks the recent calls, selects her father's number. She dials.

"Hey, Dad. You guys OK?"

"*Why's it taken so long to call with news? You want to give us a heart attack?*"

"I couldn't call before. Best you stay in hiding a bit longer. I'll stay here till I get something sorted out."

"*But we've come here to be with you.*"

"Just a few more days. When the dust settles, we can meet up."

"*No. We're a family and we're going to be together. Tell us where you are or I'm calling the police.*"

"OK, Dad, fine — don't shout. Not that any police would help you, but yeah, I guess that we're-a-family line persuaded me. I'll come to you tomorrow morning then we'll all come here."

"*Why'd we need to go there? The hotel we're at here is great. It's got a heated pool.*"

"Only you can make me laugh like that, Dad. But no. Either we stay here, or we each stay in different towns. There's a source for my story here, someone I'm going to need to meet in person a few times."

"*OK. But I bet you're in some fleapit that smells of mold and doesn't even have a pool.*"

"I'll be there early tomorrow. Goodnight, Dad. Kiss Mom for me too."

Olga turns her gaze back to her laptop screen. She opens the article and scrolls down to the last paragraphs she wrote. She looks at each line with care. The text is well structured, all the information is in place, with a partial transcript of the recording and the supporting evidence, which she will also send along as an attachment. But there's a crucial piece missing to give her journalistic work greater credibility: an interview with Preta. No matter that Chaya has forbidden Olga from talking to her. Preta's perspective, and the information she has, Olga can't get anywhere else. She's a part of the whole thing. Chaya and Preta Sarampião *are* this place, and it's Olga Befreien who will show the world who Heichma, Enrico, and the other politicians and businessmen really are, and what they could do to these women's home, the home of their great-grandfather and of all those who were born and live there. She says to herself: "I don't know how, but I am going to talk to that woman." The stuffy heat of the room is starting to get to her. She goes over to the window, opens one of the panes, then she notices a man across the street, just standing there, looking at her. He looks right at her for a few moments, then starts to move slowly away in the direction of the setting sun.

This Hell That Is Us

Late the next morning, Senna and Enrico stop the motorboat at the bank of the Uruguai River, on the Argentine side. They sit in silence, waiting, for half an hour. Preta emerges from between the trees. She's armed, with a pistol at her waist and a huge machete in her left hand. Senna is alarmed to see her, he tries to get up, loses his balance, tumbles behind the boat's wooden seat. Enrico, already on his feet, is fully alert, and notices the bandage covering a part of the woman's leg. Preta sizes Senna up.

"This the guy?" Preta takes the lead in the conversation.

"Yeah. He's chief of staff to — "

"I'm the man who's going to pay you dollars to complete a job, cabocla," Senna interrupts him, clambering out of the boat and taking two steps toward Preta.

"Cabocla?"

Preta grips the knife and advances with an agility the city boy has never seen before, stopping only when the flat of the blade is pressed to the chief of staff's neck.

"Take it easy, Preta," Enrico says.

Senna tries to explain himself:

"Uh, no offense, ma'am."

"Cabocla is a sacred word to me. Say it one more time and your tongue will be food for the palometas swimming in this river." Preta runs the back of the blade slowly down his cheek. "And don't go thinking you're talking to some dumb hick or some nobody. I know who you are, Senna, I know what you do, and I know that the job you're gonna ask me to do is for Heichma and his pals. You're just the mule who's come to bring me the message and the money. You're nobody. I could kill you right here, just say one more fucking stupid thing . . ." Preta brings the knife back to his neck, only now with the blade turned to the man's skin.

Senna doesn't reply. His teeth are chattering. His knees tremble. He pisses his pants. Preta laughs.

"Ugh, what a wimp."

"Preta, please," says Enrico. "Leave the man."

"I want to hear it from the mouth of this bedwetter, in every detail, what exactly the deputy wants me to do."

Senna tries to answer but cannot. No sound comes from his mouth.

"Let him pull himself together. He's a city boy, he's not cut out for this sort of thing," says Enrico, taking some pleasure in the words.

Preta draws the knife away from the man's neck, and he, in an impulse, backs off, then tears out into the river and grips on to the side of the boat, up to his waist in water.

"And these are the cowards who're at the top of the chain of command in this state, and in Brazil," she scoffs.

"Senna, start talking or we're never getting out of this place."

"I . . . we . . . need you to disappear . . . to dispose of the journalist," Senna says.

Enrico is incredulous.

"No, no, you said it was just to *find* the woman and get the things back from — "

"Shut up, old man! Which journalist?" Preta interrupts him.

"Olga Befreien. She was born in Dourado but she was working for the deputy . . . she worked with me in the Assembly, in Porto Alegre. She's in hiding, on this side." Senna's voice is quiet, his words halting.

"I know who she is. And why do you want to get rid of her?"

"She stole things. Really important documents. A lot of powerful people could be implicated if she showed them to anyone or told anyone about them. She needs to disappear."

"You said you just wanted to get hold of the documents," said Enrico, alarmed, "the proof."

"You know what will happen to you, to your business, and to all of us if she stays alive. Even she" — Senna points at Preta — "Could fall."

"That's not going to happen. Me and my group are invisible, we don't even exist. Isn't that right, Enrico?"

"Are you people crazy?" Enrico wakes up and walks over to Senna. "I'm not going to be complicit in a murder." He grabs the chief of staff's shirt and shoves his body into the river. The man flails.

Preta shoots into the air.

"Enough," she commands.

Old Romano lets go; Senna splutters and says hoarsely:

"Olga knows everything. It's the only way. She needs to be wiped off the map. If nobody finds the body, she'll just be a missing person and everything's resolved." Senna looks at Preta. "Isn't that how things go here?"

Enrico brings both hands to his head. He shuts his eyes and says to himself:

"Oh no, no!"

Preta spits on the ground.

"How much?"

"Twenty thousand dollars." Senna climbs out of the river and from his pocket he takes a thick folded envelope that is now soaked. "Ten today if you accept. Ten when the job is done."

"No," says Preta firmly.

Senna holds the envelope in his hand. He's confused, unsure what to do.

"I want the twenty thousand now," Preta tells him. "Or we're not discussing it."

"Preta," Enrico begs, "don't do this."

"You brought him here knowing he was bad news. Your hands are all over this already, old man, it's no use suddenly finding a conscience now," Preta says to Enrico, then she turns to Senna: "Twenty."

"I do have another two thousand here," Senna takes another envelope out from his belt, under his shirt.

"Moron." She snatches the money from him.

Preta looks with loathing and contempt at the two men. She raises the pistol and points it at Senna's forehead.

"You people don't deserve the air you breathe," she says. "You're worms."

"No, no. For God's sake. Don't do it. I have children. Small children." Senna goes back into the river and hides behind the boat. "Enrico, do something."

Enrico and Preta look hard at one another. Never moving her aim from Senna, Preta takes a few steps back, till she is at the bushes. Then she steps into the vegetation and disappears into the woods.

All for Nothing

November fifth. Olga and her parents, who are now staying at her hotel, are all having lunch. She tells them she needs to go buy cigarettes and borrows their HB20 Sport. She drives across the small town and stops outside a gas station convenience store on the western edge of the Corredera Moconá province. She fishes out a cigarette from the almost full pack in her purse and lights it, leaning on the hood. In the hope of avoiding unwanted attention, she wears sunglasses, a black cap, a long white T-shirt, jean shorts down to the knee, and flip-flops. She's just finishing her second cigarette when a motorbike carrying two women stops at one of the fuel pumps. Only the one riding pillion is wearing a helmet. The pump attendant runs over to serve them. While he fills the tank, he chats to the biker. The passenger, without removing her helmet, walks over toward Olga and, as she passes her, says quietly:

"Come with me."

Olga tosses what's left of the cigarette on the ground and follows.

"Keep walking," the woman says.

Olga does as she's told, hanging back slightly.

"We're going to walk to the end of the road. That's how much time I'm giving you."

"Thank you, Preta."

"What do you want from me?" Preta keeps walking.

"I want to give you this." Olga takes a small envelope from the pocket of her shorts and steps up the pace to give it to Preta. The woman puts it away in her bra.

"Now we can take a walk around the block. Start talking," says Preta.

They turn the corner. Olga lights another cigarette.

"It's about the wild animal meat and the wine. . . ." Olga waits for a reaction that doesn't come, so she summons up her nerve: "Some of the buyers are involved in stuff that's much worse. I've got some names, but need to confirm them with you."

Preta seems indifferent to what she is saying.

"And why would I do that?" she asks.

"Because you're Sarampião's great-granddaughter and you don't want the park under water." Olga risks playing her trump card. She manages to elicit a reaction from the Red Foot leader, who seems irritated.

"And who are you to say what I do or don't want?"

"This is only the beginning, it's a small fraction of a conspiracy involved in something worse. Bigger crimes. You're going to lose territory, Preta. That's why I'm writing this article . . . an exposé for a foreign paper. I need this interview with you. You're one of the most important names in this story."

"This is sounding like flatter to me, and I hate flattery. But seeing as you don't know me, I' gonna make one thing totally clear: Fuck this article of yours, dy, and fuck you."

An old Fiat 147 in military gre approaches slowly. From inside the car, two men look at Olga. P a raises her shirt, revealing the automatic pistol at her waist. T driver speeds up, continuing on his way. Olga looks at Preta's gu t of the corner of her eye.

"What was that?"

"That was the border land, that was what you're messing with. But you can rest easy. O am allowed to kill you here in Misiones," says Preta.

"Kill me?" asks Olga, trying le her fear.

Preta stops walking.

"I don't believe in this goo of yours, reporter girl. I don't trust anyone who comes to d rtilizer onto other people's misfortune. I don't trust anyone has no idea what it's like to live without means, to live every your life staring into the abyss."

"That's not me," says Olga, ed.

They walk on again, in sile or a few more meters.

"I want to see the names you And all those documents you got."

"How do you know about t cuments?" Olga asks.

"I know everything that ha around here. Show me or we're done talking."

Olga takes her phone o f er pocket. She unlocks it and searches for the pictures, th ds it to her.

"There are a lot more pictu here these came from, Preta," she says. "And they're kept very s n more than one location, with more than one person, on er side of the border, including with Chaya."

Preta shakes her head. She doesn't like this one bit.

"Will you work with me? Be source?" Olga insists.

"So you know who my oldest customer is, then? Who I've sold the most hunting meat to so far, right?"

"Yeah."

"I haven't seen his name on list."

"Enrico Romano's name is plenty of documents, just not these ones."

"So you're going to throw that old son of a bitch's name in too?"

Olga doesn't reply.

"You feel sorry for his son, you? You, and Chaya, and everyone else. Always covering up the corrupt Romanos. Everything swept under the rug," says Preta and then she removes her helmet. Her face and her hair are sweaty. The scars and blemishes stand out even more on the skin that's red and irritated from the potent heat. To Olga, everything about that face is extraordinary. She's fascinated. The resemblance between Preta and Chaya is striking. Apart from all the same symptoms, the most piercing thing about her is the look in her eye. It's the same as Chaya's, charged with rage and urgency.

"You guys are just the same," says Olga.

"What?"

"You and Chaya. At preschool, she didn't believe, or I didn't want to believe, that you actually existed. She talked about you so proudly, she bragged about her older cousin. I actually got envious. Now, seeing your face for the first time, the two of you are just the same." Olga turns serious. She realizes that Preta has not liked this comment.

"We have nothing in common. Not at all. This is the face of

someone who's had a life she can't imagine, that you can't imagine." She spits on the ground.

"I'm sorry. I didn't think you'd take offense."

"OK, we're done. I have nothing to say to you. Nothing to talk about, not about me or about the Red Foot."

"No, hang on — Preta, wait. It's about that too. About telling the history of you all. The story that's never been told to any newspaper before. So that your names will never be forgotten. So the decades of Red Foot history will be remembered forever. I'm sorry if I annoyed you. Enrico's name will be in there — I promise. Let me show — "

"There's already been too much blood spilled in my group's history, and on that land. You should go now, Olga," she says, her voice rougher than normal.

Olga watches Preta move away from her.

"Do whatever you like. I'm going to write about everything that happens over this side, and on the other side of the Uruguai, with or without your help. I'll just get myself some other source," she says.

Preta stops, raises her shirt, grips her gun without drawing it out of her waistband, then lunges for Olga's neck.

"I'm about one second away from using this right here."

Struggling to speak, her voice hoarse, Olga says:

"Please — just listen to me, Preta, the park's in danger, that river's in danger, the land you all live on, it's in danger. The place where Sarampião lived, your houses in Red Foot territory, it could all end up flooded."

Preta lets go of her neck.

"That hydroelectric plant is going to produce almost no energy, it'll be a total white elephant, all it'll do will be to siphon money into the pockets of those politicians and businessmen, and no one's doing anything to expose those bastards." Olga finishes her speech.

"Hey, smart-ass, big-city graduate, you think I'm an idiot?"

"No!"

"Stupid woman — I'm a *hunter*. The best here. And I know about everything that happens in this territory."

"And that's why I think you're the only person smart enough to truly see what's at stake. The only person capable of helping me get them."

"Was it Chaya who put you up to this?"

"On the contrary — she can't know I talked to you."

"Nah, this whole thing isn't adding up for me."

"What's not, Preta? I'm standing right here in front of you. Risking my life. What is it that doesn't add up?"

"Why would some girl who never respected anyone, or her hometown, who set fire to the statue of Sarampião, why would she be here risking herself to save the land where he lived?"

"People change, don't they?"

"Oh, please don't give me some corny line about redemption now, I know your type. Tell the truth. Be a woman and stop lying. What is really making you do this?" says Preta, her hand still on the gun in her waistband.

"I have reasons for wanting revenge. Satisfied? Yes, it's true, I've got a very long account I want those men to settle."

Preta claps her hands.

"Oh yes — *now* there's a real woman standing before me."

"So will you help me?"

Preta hands the envelope of money back to Olga. Her expression changes, she turns serious and says:

"I've only come here for one reason: to warn you this place is getting dangerous for you. Take your dad and your mom out of that cheap hotel and go somewhere far away. First and last warning you'll get from me."

The bike that brought Preta pulls up beside them on the street. Preta gets onto the pillion. She puts on her helmet and goes, leaving Olga behind.

Message Delivered

Afternoon of November 8. Nestor has his eyes on the laptop screen while Cláudio is at the wheel of the new Hilux, a service truck the park's been granted by the state, on a now unused road. Nestor is monitoring the signal from one of the jaguars' tracking collars. They proceed slowly, following the red dot that blinks on the screen, indicating that they are close.

"It's slowing," says Nestor. "It's around here."

They drive on, not too fast.

"It's here. She's here."

They stop and get out. Cláudio takes the rifle and Nestor the gun that shoots tranquilizer darts. Nestor walks a few more meters, alert. Above him, he sees the trepeiros attached to the tops of the trees and the bait tied to one of the trunks. He raises a clenched fist, signaling for Cláudio to stop. He continues alone, cautiously, into the forest. He spots the tracking collar tossed onto the ground. He picks it up and walks back to where Cláudio is waiting.

"It's this," Nestor shows him. "This collar was the Old Lady's. There's some blood on it — dry already."

Cláudio looks up toward where Nestor has come from, then he too spots the trepeiros.

"The Red Foot," he says, heartbroken. "Bastards."

"They left this here on purpose. A warning. We should radio Chaya to check in with her."

"No. This has got to be in person. She's going to be livid. You know how this stuff affects her."

Blood, Women, and Machetes

That same night, Chaya, with an automatic pistol in her grip and a machete at her waist, steps cautiously onto Red Foot territory. There's no one in the yard. The houses and containers have their doors and windows closed and lights off.

"Preta!" she calls out.

No answer. The only sound comes from the crickets and cicadas chirping nearby.

"Show your face, jackass!"

She hears some laughter from behind one of the containers. She points her gun in that direction:

"Who's there?"

The seconds pass with nothing happening. Until Preta, gripping a machete, appears in the darkness, behind Chaya. Her hunter's stealthy walk doesn't give her away. She stops some twenty meters away from the forest ranger.

"What took you?" Preta asks.

Chaya spins round, and as the two women face up to one another, she draws her own machete.

"Come on then!" Preta raises her blade.

Chaya lunges for her cousin, who bends her legs, draws in her stomach, concentrating her strength in her pelvis, as she learned to do from her grandmother Tédi: "*Wait till the animal is close. . . .*" Chaya gives a leap, and the two blades meet in the air. The knives strike each other two or three more times, before the women pull away and begin to circle.

"Today you're gonna take such a beating, Chaya. . . . You're gonna learn to respect the Red Foot once and for all."

"You monster! You killed our oldest jaguar."

"And you people killed one of our boys, a gunshot opened a hole in the kid's chest. You really think that I — I of all people — was going to let that pass?"

Chaya is disoriented.

"I . . . I didn't know . . ."

"Aw, poor little orphan, no one ever tells her anything. Nothing is ever her fault."

"You piece of shit, you go ahead, make a joke, just like you joke about any hurt you've ever caused. . . . After what you did to my grandpa, I shouldn't have expected anything from you but more and more death."

"Arrê! Armin's death wasn't my fault, Chaya, come on."

"He could have lived a few years longer if you hadn't . . ."

"If I hadn't what? If I hadn't defended myself?"

"So you'll justify your crimes with lies?"

"What you call a crime, I call *survival*."

Chaya looks at Preta's rigid face and body, the rage in her eyes. Suddenly, as though understanding the real reason she had been brought here, she asks:

"So — it was you?"

"You used to be quicker than that, Chaya."

"It was you people who set fire to the park."

Preta laughs. Chaya's blade slices into her cousin's shoulder. Preta lets out a howl — but then smiles, yes, she likes it, she wants this fight, she turns her body and attacks. This time she kicks her cousin in the belly, and Chaya falls, but soon she's up again, one hand clenching her stomach.

"You don't deserve to have Sarampião's blood running through you. . . ."

"That old crap again . . ." Preta cuts her own left forearm, and lets the blood trickle down till it reaches her hand and fingers. She rubs it on her face, over her eyes and mouth. "His shitty old blood has taken more from us than it's ever given."

"You do what you do because there's wickedness inside you, Preta."

"As wicked as your snitch of a grandpa."

"Bitch, you shut that trap of yours. . . ."

Chaya makes another cut in the Red Foot leader's arm. Her attack was so swift that Preta is enraged at her own inability to defend herself. With the pain triggering her adrenaline, she strikes back, a relentless onslaught until she has made a wound in Chaya's leg. Chaya drops to her knees.

"If that's how it's gonna be, we keep going till it's over," Preta warns her.

"I tried to forgive you. For Sarampião. And I regret it now." Chaya struggles back to her feet. Preta walks over to her. The two bodies meet. Their breasts and foreheads press against one another. The blood of one mingles with the blood of the other on the dry earth. Exhausted, panting, they study one another. Now Chaya takes a step back and, without a second thought, draws her gun and points.

"Weakling." Preta spits on the ground.

From the darkness, from between the houses, a couple of women emerge with .44 rifles trained on Chaya.

"You can all back off," says Preta. "This is between the two of us."

Preta and Chaya are still facing one another.

"How could you? Sarampião is there! That was his home, it still is, and you tried — " starts Chaya, but she's interrupted.

"He doesn't have a home."

"He does. You know he does. Our moms saw it. You and I did, we both saw it."

"Kids' stuff."

A gust of warm wind blows between the two of them. Chaya understands what it means. Preta does too, though she won't acknowledge it.

They look up, to the tops of the trees, to the branches swaying. Clouds are appearing in the starless sky. Preta stretches out her arm, splays a hand, and feels the hot wind passing through her fingers. She drops her knife.

The first drops of rain begin to fall on them. They hear a moan coming from inside the forest. And then a whisper:

"Help. I'm . . ."

A bloodied woman appears from between the trees, staggers out into the rain.

Chaya and Preta can't see much in the darkness, but as the

woman approaches, they realize her hands are bound with duct tape. She totters toward Chaya. Her face is covered in bruises and her eyes are swollen. Her arms and legs have visible cuts on them.

"Olga?" says Chaya. The journalist's body bends, then drops into the forest ranger's arms. "Olga, what happened?"

Preta rushes over. She and Chaya pick up the journalist and carry her into the house. They lay her down on the ground, propped up against a wall. The rain outside is getting heavier.

"What happened?" Chaya tries to talk to Olga, who doesn't answer. "Was this you?" she snaps at Preta. "How did she wind up here?"

"Don't underestimate me, Chaya. If I wanted your friend dead, she'd be dead." Preta takes Olga's face in her hand. "Who did this to you? Tell me, who was it, who had the arrogance to disobey me?"

"Disobey you? What are you talking about?" Chaya gives her cousin a shove.

Olga tries to communicate:

"There was . . . a tree trunk . . . car . . . Beating, with sticks . . . on my back, my head."

"Hey, I'm right here with you." Chaya cuts the tape around Olga's wrists.

"Take me out of . . ." Olga begs her.

"I'm going to put whoever did this in the ground," Preta yells.

"We're getting out of here," says Chaya.

"No!" says Preta. "No one can leave this place. Least of all her."

The storm passes, as do the hours. Preta emerges from a room in the house carrying an aluminum bucket full of water, macerated leaves, and a bloodstained piece of cloth. She heads for the kitchen, where Chaya, with a bit of fabric tied around the cut on her leg, sits wordlessly. The expression on the face of the Red Foot leader is death.

"Is she . . . ?" Chaya can't finish her question.

"She's alive," replies Preta. "And she's gonna live."

The two women hear footsteps approaching. Chaya draws her gun. Preta takes a knife from the drawer at the sink beside her. Thales appears in the doorway. He runs over to hug Chaya.

"Just as well you managed to get word to me," he says. "Where is she?"

Leaning beside a window in Preta's kitchen, Thales looks out at the pitch blackness of the night. He's crying.

"I'm so sorry," says Chaya. "If I could have, I never would have brought you into this whole mess. But there was no way it could stay hidden any longer. I'm worried about you. You've got to keep away from Enrico. There's a net closing round him. It'll get dangerous for you too. Do you understand, Thales?" she asks.

Thales doesn't reply.

"Enough secrets. You're my brother and I'll always be by your side and I'll help with whatever you need, but you got to keep away from him."

Thales wipes his face and looks at his sister.

"You're right, sis — and now we've got nothing to lose. Neither of us. Which is why it's time you knew the truth too." He points at Preta. "You and her."

In a Family, What's Hidden Should Stay Hidden

Gringa Romano walked ahead, Armin right behind her, looking grim. They entered the house and took their places in the living room, each eyeing the other warily. Gringa offered Armin the sofa, but he didn't accept. The woman took the lead: Did Roscato tell you? How do you know I went to see my brother, Gringa? Oh, buddy, I know a lot. So tell me if Caco said he and Roscato saw our dad when they killed that jaguar? Silence. Hand Roscato over to me, and I'll tell you what I know. Armin walked up to Gringa and said threateningly: Tell me what happened to Sarampião. I don't care how much you're suffering, I swear I will kill you if you lay a hand on me, Gringa warned him. Armin stepped back. If you know what happened, Gringa, just tell me — please? Look, pal, nothing comes for free, Roscato's gotta pay — you promise? Armin agreed. Sarampião was on Mad Mouth's tail that day, just like Caco and Roscato were. Your brother fired two shots to kill the jaguar. One hit her. The second didn't. Your father, in some way that Caco wasn't able to explain, appeared from behind a bush and positioned himself in front of the animal. What're you saying woman? Roscato and Caco ran through the scrub to where your father and the animal had fallen, but when they got there they only found the jaguar down, and blood on the ground. Sarampião vanished. Armin's hands and arms were quivering like leaves. His face seemed to have sagged, as if he'd aged thirty years in those few minutes. A moment of discomfort settled slowly between them. Now tell me: where's your brother? Armin gave up Roscato's whereabouts to Gringa. The agreement between the two of them was that the tragedy involving Sarampião would never be told to anyone. The shame of the whole business was something neither of them wanted to ever see the light of day. In a family, what's hidden should stay hidden.

Preta takes a glass from off the table and hurls it against the wall. Holding her knife, she starts to move toward Thales.

"It was him, that old son of a bitch, was it him who told you this lie?"

"No more lies, Preta."

Her strength fades, she drops the knife. She feels like she's suffocating. She stumbles out of the house and falls.

"Did he kill him? Did he kill Sarampião? Did my grandpa Roscato kill him? What about Tédi? Did Tédi know?" Preta says over and over, staring at the wet red mud.

Without coming too close, Chaya watches her cousin and realizes that she doesn't feel anything at all, not sadness, not pity, not rage. Nothing. Preta kneels in front of her, cradling her head. She starts to cry, till she's sobbing. Chaya understands that, this time, Preta doesn't have anywhere or anyone to target her rage at, no one against whom to take revenge. All that's left is a past filled with mistakes and with blood that the two women never imagined they'd have to contend with.

Chaya looks up at the sky. Th stars and the moon have appeared. Preta gradually composes h self and gets up. She and Chaya are finally meeting in the same pla in the tragedy that has been pursuing the Sarampiãos for dec s and which has punished them, destroying the possibility of a together, as the family's only two survivors. They have borne th onsequences of choices made by people who are no longer in th world.

Chaya, her expression hard someon in turmoil, says firmly:

"Now, Olga will stay here the's safe and strong. Th les will notify her parents. I'll get Olga's appearance announced on some radio stations and in a few n apers. They'll think they've succeeded. That they've finished off. That they've won. And you, Preta, you'll tell her whatever needs to finish her exposé for the paper. If we can't get back at th who harmed us in the past, we'll go after those doing it now. And 're getting them all."

The day dawns. Preta, still smeared in mud and blood, is in the yard, along with a group of other Red Foot women, standing at a bucket. She is holding a clean cloth. She takes off her clothes till she is totally naked. One of the women throws the greenish liquid over her head.

Arrê. Preta shuts her eyes and continues.

Oh caboclo, Arrê.

With the cloth, she begins to wash her cuts.

Protect the Turvo

Altar place of everything.

She washes her body. She washes away the weakness she feels.

Faith-man

In the forest

Cure the land

Cure the water

Cure it Sarampião.

Olga appears in the doorway of the house and watches her from afar. Preta drops the stained cloth into the bucket. She looks down at the cloudy water inside.

"One of us women is going to die," she says to herself.

The Sins of the Father

Thales returns to Dourado, having spent the rest of the day in Corredera Moconá, at the hotel where Olga's parents are staying, trying to calm them down, assuring them that their daughter is safe and that in a few days she'd be back with them again. One of the Red Foot women, who had gone with him, was standing guard.

He drives down Avenida das Viuvinhas. He feels a kind of physical and mental paralysis he's never experienced before. In order to keep himself alert, he switches on the radio: "Olga Befreien was born in the town of Dourado. The missing journalist was last seen . . ."

He turns it off again.

Arriving at the corner where the Jaguar Hotel is located, he spots two cars, one from the civil police and the other from the military brigade, along with the town ambulance, all parked outside the hotel. He abandons his own car in the middle of the road and runs. He's blocked by Dóris, in uniform.

2007

What Doesn't Hurt the Other

Blame, Truth, Lies

Early morning. Thales is driving his father's 4x4. Fito Paez's "A rodar mi vida" blasting on the radio Olga, gripping a bottle of wine, rolls down the window, leans half her body out and yells:

"Wake up, Dourado! Take a look at the most spectacular journalist-to-be in all Rio Grande do Sul!"

Thales grabs the waistband of Olga's pants and pulls her back inside.

"Think you might have attracted enough attention yet? The police'll show up and put a stamp on your future and you'll never get to be a journalist at all."

"It does look like those fucking pigs are awake."

"Well, you've woken up one of the residents — look, there, that light's on . . ."

"Fuck it — a few months from now I'm going to be living in Porto Alegre for real."

"Yeah, but I'll still be here, Olga. And I'm the one driving without a license."

"Ah, Mr. Goody-Two-Shoes. Just like his sister. You can't see anything beyond this town. You people can all kiss my ass."

Olga drinks directly from the bottle until the liquid spills out of her mouth and over her chin and onto her lap, staining her shirt.

"Oh, shit."

"You're drunk. I'm taking you home."

They drive past the square.

"Stop the car."

"No. I'm taking you away."

Olga opens the door. Thales brakes. She totters out, the bottle of wine still in her hand. She feels the chill of the icy air and zips up her red velvet jacket. She crosses the street in the low fog and stops in front of the statue of Sarampião.

"Dumbass statue . . . That old dumbass . . ."

Thales takes the bottle from her.

"This silly grudge of yours against Chaya and her family has gotten ridiculous. Stop being a child."

"Grudge? She humiliated me, said horrible things to me. That cow hates me." Olga takes back the bottle and walks away from him.

"Well, you're the one who started it this time. So you can stop playing the victim."

"She was fooling around with that girl from out of town. I saw her opening her blouse, pulling off her bra . . . I just made a tiny comment. What's the problem?"

"Saying Chaya kisses men but what she really likes is hooking up with women in secret? That's just a tiny comment?"

Olga doesn't answer.

"You know what the problem is, looking from outside?" Thales goes on. "It's that you seem to find her life more interesting than your own."

"Jerk . . ."

"She's my sister! You just do such crazy shit, Olga. You keep reaching new lows. . . . Why were you even following Chaya, anyway?"

Olga pours a large amount of wine into her mouth and spits it in the face of the Sarampião statue.

"You always had some kind of prejudice against her."

Olga interrupts him.

"Enough! I can't take any more of this. So when *she's* the prejudiced one, oh, that's just fine then, is it? When she's aggressive — just fine! Everyone here feels sorry for her. No one dares to criticize her. Am I the only person who can see how Sarampião's great-grandkid thinks she's better than all the rest of us?"

"Man, you're obsessed . . ."

"*I'm* obsessed? She can't even look at me when . . . She can't accept that we're together, you and me, didn't she say I wasn't right for you? Chaya can't see us happy because *she's* not happy. And that's the truth."

"This is all in your head."

"You tell me, Thales — you think she's rooting for our relationship? Or does she keep coming up with new things to try to turn you against me?"

Thales doesn't answer.

"Do you really love me?" Olga asks. "Or are you just passing the time?"

"Oh, come on. . . . You know I'm crazy about you."

"So prove it."

"I have, haven't I?"

"Prove it by taking my side, not Chaya's."

Olga goes back to the car. She opens the trunk and takes out a hose, then an empty bottle. She opens the fuel tank. She puts the hose inside and sucks on the end. Nothing comes out. She tries again. A bit of gas gets into her mouth. She spits it out. She fills the bottle with the liquid, and walks back to the statue. She picks up the wine again, rinses out her mouth, drinks, then smashes that bottle at Sarampião's feet.

"Stop this, Olga, you're gonna hurt yourself."

Thales tries to restrain her.

"Either you take my side now or we're over."

Olga pours the gas over the statue. She takes a cigarette and lighter from inside her jacket. She lights the cigarette, draws on it once, twice, then hands it to Thales.

"Go on, then. Throw it."

Thales doesn't move. He just stares at the ember. Olga takes the cigarette from his hand and drops it to the ground. The fire begins timidly but grows till it's a huge flame covering the entire concrete statue. Then everything around it starts to burn.

"You've gone mad. Oh, God . . ." Thales grabs Olga's arm and they run toward the car. "We've got to get out of here before they catch us."

They hear the siren of a military police car. Within seconds, the red glow of the spinning beacon is reflecting in their faces.

Faith

December Gifts

It's the start of December, and Olga's investigative report is finally published in *El País*, then reproduced on various Brazilian websites before spreading right across the world. In a matter of hours, it finds its way into the headlines and reverberates through Brazil's press and social media like a bomb. The posts from internet users couldn't be more varied:

> "Journalist believed dead comes back to life to dispense justice."

> "Olga Befreien comes for the upper echelons of government with her exposé of corruption in a small Rio Grande do Sul town."

> "Politicians with links to the Presidential Palace say the word 'impeachment' is once again haunting the President of the Republic."

Users share not only the details of the case but also the evidence implicating people associated with the federal government, businessmen, and politicians from São Paulo and Rio Grande do Sul as well as Argentina.

Olga, sitting at her computer in a hotel room, lights a cigarette, closes the browser tabs of the social media sites, and opens the pages for the country's main newspapers.

> According to the journalist, it all began with illegal fishing and hunting, along with the illicit transporting of Argentine wines to evade duty. Behind it: bribes, kickbacks, dispossession of lands . . .

> In Brazil, only 12% of the Atlantic forest biome is still standing. All the rest has been deforested. If this binational venture is approved, much of what remains of it in the south of the country is at risk of disappearing.

> The current head of the Turvo park, Chaya Sarampião, pointed out that the place is the final refuge of the jaguar anywhere in the south of Brazil. She claimed that the local community has never been in favor of the hydroelectric plant and they were attempting to prove the irregularities in the documentation being presented.

One anonymous source of Befreien's, who lives across the border, had actually negotiated directly with some of the names on the list of those involved, and was able to corroborate.

Federal Supreme Court judge Petrus da Silva, who lifted the confidentiality restrictions on the banking information of Acício Vilmar Senna, chief of staff to deputy Afrânio Heichma, of the NEP (the National Environmental Party), made these documents public. They revealed hundreds of monthly deposits of two thousand reals, fractional sums that could pass unnoticed by the scrutiny of the Central Bank. It was the money from the so-called "rachadinhas," portions of the salaries of the employees at the office where Olga Befreien worked and whose activities she exposed. The journalist managed to secure evidence, recordings . . .

The businessmen and politicians involved in the hunting, buying, and selling of wild animals are the very same ones implicated in the falsification of documents and the deliberate overpricing of the Gran Roncador Binational Hydroelectric Dam—a project that the current federal government insisted on dusting off when they assumed the presidency. Among countless irregularities, an untruthful and misleading environmental impact study (EIS) claimed that the Yucumã Falls, the widest waterfall in the world, would not be affected. The Federal University of Rio Grande do Sul

(URFGS), together with local universities, have presented entirely different conclusions in their EIS's, as revealed in Befreien's article, demonstrating that a genuine environmental crime would be committed if Gran Roncador were to be built.

"So there we are," says Olga, "you assholes are well and truly fucked now."

The Reality of Chaos

That same morning, Heichma and Senna are in the office, where the phones are ringing off the hook.

"Shameless fucking bitch! She recorded me! That bitch recorded me!" splutters Heichma.

"We're gonna deny everything, Deputy Heichma," says Senna, trying to appear sober. He drank four shots of whiskey at home, at breakfast, as soon as he started reading the news.

"You told me she was dead!" says Heichma, giving Senna a shove. Senna staggers, crashing into the wall.

"Whoa, you lost your mind? What the hell?"

"That's nothing *close* to what those Brasília folks are gonna do to you." Heichma picks up one of the phones from the desk and hurls it as Senna's face. Senna puts up his hands to shield himself.

"It's not my fault. They assured me it was done."

"You are so stupid, Senna — so very stupid. Hiring teenagers to do adult work."

"It's all there was. No adult was brave enough to disobey that cabocla."

Heichma walks over to the window. "I need to think."

Then he strides back to the desk and sits down. He's trying, desperate, to find some way to save himself and to derail the political and social lynching that has already begun. He picks up his phone:

"I want you to get the other lawyers together, and for all of you to meet me at the apartment in half an hour." He hangs up. "Senna, tell Ana Paula to go home and to shut the whole place up. No one answers the phones, no one talks to the media."

Senna is confused.

"And what do I do, deputy?"

"You? You take your things and never come back. And don't call me. The lawyers are going to compose a statement clarifying that you take personal responsibility for all these charges. It'll go out in the press tomorrow."

The Marks of Time

Late that morning, Thales is in the hotel office sitting behind what used to be his father's desk. He is analyzing old and new accounting paperwork. He receives a message from a friend with a link, and opens it: "*Businessmen and politicians from the town of Dourado, at the state's northwestern border, are also involved.*"

The phone keeps on receiving messages, one after another. He puts it down. The beeping continues. His thin, pale face looks old.

Early afternoon. Maurício Ricci is in the town's working-class neighborhood, parked on the road that ends at the local public school bearing his name. He's holding a two-page supplement from the newspaper *Notícias Noroeste*:

As the proof unearthed by Olga Befreien showed, Claudenir Ricci, Dourado's former mayor and founding member of the National Environmental Party, as well as his son, Maurício Ricci, are two of the businessmen named in the the chief of staff's ledger.

"Fucking whores." He punches the roof of the car.

The day is drawing to a close. At the Turvo park HQ, Cláudio, Nestor, two colleagues from the admin center, and a guard are all celebrating.

"There's gonna be some people sleeping on the concrete tonight," says Nestor, with a laugh.

"You reckon?" asks the guard who's getting ready to begin her shift.

"No way for them to deny their dirty tricks now. And the people here who're mixed up in it, you know they never fooled me," says Nestor, his expression serious.

Chaya comes in.

"OK, let's get on with our chores, soldiers. Each one of us deals with their tasks. It's gonna be a long night for us here at the park. And listen up—we've won the battle, but not the war. The Turvo still needs us."

"My shift's done, boss," says Cláudio. "I'm gonna stop by Lieutenant Ângelo's. He must be pretty cheerful at the news."

"Lieutenant Ângelo isn't in the town anymore. Transferred."

"What do you mean, boss?"

"It was in the Official Gazette," says Chaya. "He moved to the admin center in Porto Alegre."

"He left? Without saying goodbye to us?" Cláudio is disappointed at the news.

"The Environment Ministry notified me early today."

They exchange a glance, then Cláudio lowers his eyes.

"Not everything is as it seems, Cláudio. Specially not here in the Turvo. Now, let's get to it. I've got a lot of work to do."

Rotten Meat

December 23, 2019. Seven thirty in the morning. Olga is watching a Brazilian news bulletin on her laptop, in her hotel room in Corredera Moconá. She's looking at pictures of the federal police leaving Senna's house. He's handcuffed, in a light-gray T-shirt and sweatpants, wearing a white cap. Under the pictures are the words: *Operation Rotten Meat — chief of staff to Dep. Heichma arrested in greater Porto Alegre.* The anchor reads: "The chief of staff, one of the scheme's architects, is currently being placed under arrest. As we reported earlier, arrests are also under way in São Paulo and Brasília. Meanwhile, in the town of Dourado, where the conservation area of the Turvo State Park is located, former Mayor Ricci and his son were not found. Politicians from parties that make up the national government have not been taken, nor Deputy Heichma, as in keeping with the prerogatives of parliamentary immunity, but according to the opposition, petitions will be filed requesting that this immunity be withdrawn for all those involved."

The same report shows a video of Olga, replaying an online interview from some days earlier.

"When they start locking this gang up, when the Turvo and the Yucumã Falls are safe, I'll feel it's safe for me to return to Brazil. I don't regret anything, but my family and I need to remain in hiding." The banner reads: *Olga Befreien — journalist who exposed crimes that led to operation Rotten Meat.*

Olga knows that she and her family will have no peace and will not be totally safe if they return now. But neither she nor her parents can bear to stay in that hotel in Argentina any longer. Thales had already offered rooms at the Jaguar, and Chaya in her house, as well as an improvised security escort, men she trusts, at least for the first few days. Both of them argue that the entire town is grateful to the journalist, and she and her family will be well protected there.

She shuts the computer. She lifts the phone off the hook and calls through to the next-door room.

"Time to go back. We're leaving here tomorrow."

His Own Poison

That same day, early afternoon, a scorching heat beats down on the Red Foot. The relative humidity is low, which over the last couple of decades has increasingly become the norm this late in the year. No one works at this time. Instead, everyone has retired for a siesta, to return to their toil after four o'clock. Everyone, that is, except Preta, who hasn't been able to shut her eyes. She sits under the canopy of a large tree where she prepares the leaf bath in a bowl, mashing rue leaves, Brazilian boldo, and rosemary. Everyone will wash themselves with it at the festivities leading up to Christmas Eve. Sweat trickles down the nape of her neck to her coccyx. She puts her hair up in a bun. Two banana toucans settle on a branch and for a moment she's distracted by their brilliant plumage.

León appears before her.

"Why aren't you having a siesta?" she asks.

"*Yo quiero que . . .*"

"Not in Spanish here. I've told you before."

"I want to know why."

Preta points at him, her finger dripping in the brownish-green liquid. "Because this is just how it has to be from now on. We're not killing any more animals. We're not going into the park to kill anything," and she resumes her macerating of the leaves.

"*You* taught us this, we always live like this. *Es nuestro trabajo.*"

"Well, we do different work now. There are some things that need to change, León."

"Because you and her decided, *tú y tu prima*?"

"No!" Preta drops the leaves in the bowl and looks straight at him. "Something bigger — destiny — decided."

"I thought you were la jefa of everything here, no?"

Preta doesn't answer.

"You got humiliated for her. You humiliated us. And instead you choose tu prima, your cousin from la policía! Tédi never would do that. When I'm jefe of the Red Foot, we go back to being what we always been: hunters. And I'll spit on your tumba." León spits on the ground and then looks hard at Preta, his face transformed, as if it were no longer him who was here.

The hair on her arms stands on end. She hears echoes of someone else in that look, in that speech. She puts one of her hands over her mouth, her eyes widen.

"No!" she says.

She takes a fistful of crushed wet leaves, goes over to the boy, grips his neck, and then rubs his mouth, then his face. The boy cries out and coughs up green drool.

"That's enough! Enough of this insane thirst for blood! Sarampião and the rest of my family will rest, your father will rest. And you, León, you need some possibility for a future. You can't stay here anymore. You just can't." Preta goes back to the bench, places her hands on it, and lowers her head, searching for a solution.

"Ay, you were never valiente like Tédi," he says.

Preta kicks the bench, which flies aside, and in the blink of an eye, she's on top of León, slapping his face. He falls to the floor. His nose is bleeding.

"Don't talk about things you don't understand. Don't talk about things you've never experienced. I brought you up since you were a kid. Many here would say, like a son. But remember: You are not my son. You're nothing to do with me. Nothing to do with anyone here."

"You, you . . . go . . . *ándate a la concha de tu madre*!" León spits. "Go fuck yourself!" He runs off.

A woman with a swollen face and sweaty disheveled hair hurries out in time to see León go.

"That one, he's been troubled for some time."

Other people from the community emerge. Preta gestures for them to go back to their rest. They obey.

"The little shit, he's filling the heads of the other teens with bad ideas," says the woman, the only one who has not left.

"He's gone too far, I know."

"He's changed. He's not the same León I knew. He has this fury, some really bad thing that's poisoning that head of his. It's not something that can be fixed."

"Morning, my love! Did you sleep well? Just to let you know we're coming over on the last crossing. Go wait for us with my car, could you? I can't handle going around in Senhor Befreien's anymore, or with him. And we're gonna bring something for Christmas at Chaya's. Don't bother telling me we don't need to, no way we're showing up empty handed. Maybe something from here in Argentina? Some turrón? A hunk of beef to grill? Would you let me know? Lots of love."

She turns on the car radio and lets the music play.

The Collector of Weapons and Regrets

Nine a.m. A lovely, pleasant day has dawned over the Red Foot settlement. Everyone's taking care of their chores. Men sweep the yard with besoms made of tree branches. A group of elderly people hang Christmas decorations on the surrounding trees, while another group drapes cables of colored blinking lights between the houses. Children and adolescents are peeling cassavas. Two women open bags of ice, emptying them into a metal pot to chill bottles of Fernet and Coca-Cola. Women and men paint the outside of the homes with paint that Preta has bought, something that hasn't been done in a long time. They crack jokes and chat among themselves. Four adolescents, two girls and two boys aged fourteen or fifteen, sit a bit apart from the rest, washing the peeled cassavas in plastic buckets. They have a dog with them. The animal stares into the forest and suddenly begins to growl and bark. They turn to look, then one of the girls runs over, calling out "Olga!"

"How lovely this place is looking." Olga kisses the girl's forehead. The dog starts wagging its tail. She allows it to lick her face.

"You really are impossible." Preta appears beside them. The two women hug.

"I needed to say goodbye to everyone," Olga says.

"Your call was enough. You know it's still not safe for you to be going about alone around here."

"I don't give a fuck about Heichma. They won't intimidate me. Not anymore. Anyway, I can defend myself now." Olga lifts the hem of her shirt to show her gun. Preta laughs.

"So you've turned gunslinger now? Girl, when'd that happen?"

"Don't underestimate me, Preta."

"Underestimate you? Never again."

All the adolescents hug Olga. The people of the community pause their chores and come over. They greet the journalist respectfully.

"I owe you all so much . . ."

Olga is interrupted by Preta.

"Let's do without the sentimentality. Please."

An armed woman, sweating and out of breath, comes over to the group.

"Find him?" asks Preta.

"He got away. He's real nimble," she says.

Preta looks back to the group of teenagers, who are totally silent. She stares at each in turn, up close to their faces. She stops in front of one of the boys and pulls his ear upward — he stands with his tiptoes barely touching the ground, protesting at the pain.

"Where is he?"

"No sé, I ain't seen him."

The other three teenagers stare at Preta.

She lets go of one boy and she's onto the other. She grabs a handful of hair on the side of his head, but this one shows neither fear nor pain. She slaps him. His expression doesn't change. She does it again, even harder now. He laughs and makes a gun with two fingers and mimes firing it. Rushing to her house, she bounds up the wooden steps and goes through the kitchen to her bedroom. An old wooden box sits on top of the dresser, the only thing she brought from Dourado, a memento from a time when she didn't yet have any idea of the cruelty of this world. The padlock is broken. Nothing's inside. The old .32 caliber she bought when she was still young, her first gun, is gone. She hurls the box against the wall and returns to the yard, wild at the awareness that, on top of everything, her prediction might come true.

She grabs the same boy, this time by the neck, and squeezes, making no attempt to hold back.

"Where has he gone?"

He can't answer, his face turning red.

"I'm going to pull out every one of your fingers, all of you, if you don't talk. I swear I will," she says to the other teenagers, who start to cry.

"For God's sake, they're just children," says Olga, who steps in and takes hold of one of Preta's arms, but Preta shoves her aside then throws the boy to the ground.

"Everybody shut up," Preta orders.

The same boy whom Preta almost choked is the one who hazards a justification:

"He'll kill us if we tell."

Preta draws a gun from the back of her waistband, grabs the dog, who's in the middle of the group, and points at the animal's belly — it squeals, trying to escape.

One of the girls begs: "No, por favor!"

"One, two . . ." Preta starts to count.

"Across the river. Next to the falls." The boy says this loud, trying to make his voice audible over the shrill noise coming from the dog.

"In the park?" asks Preta, and the boy on the ground confirms this.

Preta lets go of the animal, and the boy takes it in his arms. Olga looks in horror at the leader of the group, who reaches into her shorts pocket and pulls out a small old cell phone. She makes a call.

"Shit. It's turned off."

"Preta, what's going on?"

"Get your phone. Try calling Chaya," Preta shouts hoarsely.

"What's wrong? Call her why?"

"We need to find Chaya."

León

For my papá.”

Cloudy Water

After leaving Red Foot, Preta and I took the boat, crossed the river, ran through the woods till we reached the crags where the falls begin. We proceeded across that sea of basalt rocks, and then saw Chaya far off in the distance, really far off. She seemed to be staggering as she walked. Maybe she was injured, or just exhausted. Sunstroke maybe, the sun was hot that morning. We heard the crack of gunshots, and she threw herself to the ground and hid behind one of the taller rocks. That was when we saw León. He was armed. It all happened so fast. Just seconds. He shot again in Chaya's direction. Preta yelled, I yelled. We called her name several times. But the sound of the Uruguai, the sound of the Yucumã Falls . . . there was no way she could hear us. We ran as fast as we could. Preta fired in the direction of the boy, first just to scare him, then not. But he was still there. Chaya got up again and came out from behind the rock. She stood in front of León. That was when the sun's reflection flashed in the water, blinding us for a moment. Just the tiniest moment. And we heard another shot. When we were able to see again, Chaya was no longer there. She was no longer there. León ran to the right, toward the forest. Instinctively I went left, toward the river. Preta followed me. We reached the bank and glimpsed Chaya almost submerged, trying to swim amid the strong currents from the violent falls. She looked like she was being swallowed. I shouted while Preta held me back. This was wrong. It wasn't real. It couldn't be real. You understand? As if the prayer of this-isn't-happening just made sense, her, she of all people, bathed in blood, submerged in the Uruguai River. Chaya was still beating her arms. I tried to throw myself in to help her. Chaya was the one who'd saved me, she'd saved me from the person I used to be, I couldn't give up on her. . . . But Preta held me back. If she hadn't held me back . . . I tried to pull free, I scratched her hands, hit her face, but Preta clung to my body with all her strength and didn't let go. We saw the water carry Chaya away. "She's the best swimmer I know. She's gonna make it, she's gonna make it, she is," Preta was saying while I tried to think of some way to reverse it. To turn back time.

"Do you remember anything else? Do you know which way León went? Do you know whose gun it was he was carrying?"

She is alive, isn't she? No body, no death. That's what you said, madam delegate. That was it, senhora — you said: No body, no death.

Yucumã Moconá, "The Great Snorer Who Swallows Everything"

December 24, 2020. Carrying flowers and candles, men and women appear on the track, just past the end of the road that visitors use, which runs through the conservation area. They are headed toward the Yucumã Falls. Being an open space, not everybody is wearing a face mask, now compulsory for those entering the park.

Thales and Dóris follow closely behind; Cláudio and Nestor and three rangers are with them, along with a couple of guards. Masks cover their mouth and nose.

"How're you doing, Thales?" asks Dóris.

"Worn out," he replies. "A year without her, but it feels like ten, or twenty. I searched so much, this river, this forest . . . I know what I need to do now is summon up the strength to preserve her legacy and name, but it's just too hard."

"You'll manage — and everyone here in Dourado, we're all here to help you," says the police officer.

"Us from the park too," adds Cláudio.

"Thank you. You recovered OK, Cláudio?" Thales asks.

"Oh, man — I've never seen an illness like it. Ten days on oxygen, another three weeks at home in bed. I still get short of breath when I'm on a longer walk through the bush — but I couldn't not be here for . . ." Cláudio stops talking. He sees that Thales's eyes are misty.

"You know, I still see her in her uniform, walking around the place, whenever I come here."

"We do too, Thales," says Nestor. "It's like she might just appear any moment from between the trees or inside the HQ. A moment, two, then I look to one side and I think she's blown past like the wind, the way she used to. I even hear her voice giving us orders."

They reach the others on the riverbank. The growling of the falls and the violence of the water are greater than normal. Some people drop their flowers into the Uruguai, others place them down on the ground, on the rocks. The candles in everybody's hands are lit. Despite the breeze, none of them go out.

Olga is alone in a small motorboat. She crosses the river. Expertly she holds the tiller and steers through the currents as if she's been doing this her whole life. She reaches the far side and moors, tying the small craft to a tree close to the bank. Her boots sink ankle-deep in the muddy earth. Following the trail, she climbs the steep bank, holding on to the tree roots and branches. At the crest of the hill, she catches sight of a hawk-eagle at the top of a tree. It calls out, then takes flight. She follows it along the horizon until it disappears into the vastness of the Uruguai River. Then she lets her eyes rest on the Turvo park.

"You really needed to choose this place?" Preta appears, her feet and legs similarly muddy.

Olga turns with a smile. She takes a mask out of her back pants pocket, puts it on, and goes over to hug her friend.

"Still using those things?" Preta says, goading her.

"And why aren't you?"

"That pandemic hasn't reached us here. I hope it never does."

"Another reason why I should be wearing this when I'm around you. I was in São Paulo last week — place is totally overwhelmed."

"You were doing that TV program, right? We managed to see a few bits. You talking about Heichma's arrest. Made me proud."

"Took a while to get him, but yeah. Couldn't have happened without you."

"All three of us."

Olga lowers her eyes to the ground.

"But I'm not buying all that crap about him staying under house arrest," Preta goes on.

"The pandemic will be over soon, and so will his resources. He'll be off to the Charqueadas prison."

The two women watch the river current for a few moments.

"A year," says Olga.

"A year."

"You still looking for her, Preta?"

"We stopped our search some time ago."

"I went out to look for Chaya down the river every week of this — "

"I know," Preta interrupts her. "You don't need to tell me you never gave up on her."

"Not a single item of clothing, a cap, a boot, a gun . . . Nothing. You said yourself, these things can take time, but you do always find *something*. Just to be totally sure . . ."

"I am sure, Olga."

A gust of warm wind blows past them. Preta opens her arms wide. Olga watches, then copies her.

"Arrê!" they both say.

Olga wanders off, pensive. She doesn't believe that real life can be merely waiting. Pain that stands still just grows and wounds.

"She just *left*? Just like that?" asks Olga softly, talking inwardly as if not wanting an answer.

"No, Chaya, she never left. Your eyesight is still cloudy, that's all. Clear it. She's there," Preta points at the river, "and she's there," she points at the forest.

Olga looks around her, then at the stretch of track she's just climbed, and then she holds out her hand to Preta. "Come out on the boat with me. Let's go look for her. One last time."

Exú killed a bird yesterday,
with a stone he threw today.

— Yoruba saying

Láròyè Mo juba
Odò Ìyá
Òóré Yèyè ó
Òké Aro
Ògún Yè

Acknowledgments

To Paulo Scott, my love, for the support, for having been the first person to say I needed to write this story, and for his countless readings.

To Stéphanie Roque, my editor, for her brilliance and dedication from the very start, for having constructed *Água turva — The Red Earth* — with me. And also to Luiz Schwarcz, for his careful reading and detailed suggestions.

To Emanuel Kretzmann, "for having held the knife" to protect us. For having been with me, countless times, on field trips in the Turvo park.

To Ronaldo Costa, environmental analyst at ICMBIO/MMA, former head of the Taim Ecological Station, for his reading and for guidance on technical matters that were crucial to the book.

To Daniel Kretzmann, zootechnician, for his guidance on the species of fish in the Uruguai River and the feeding of the animals that are in the Turvo State Park.

To Aline Bei, Carola Saavedra, and Jeferson Tenório for the words that are too big to fit inside me.

Acknowledgments

To Marcelino Freire and Valeria Lamego, for their readings of the book and their unconditional friendship. Also to Andréa del Fuego, Luiz Antonio de Assis Brasil, Yuti Al'Hanati, Rodrigo Lacerda, Cíntia Moscovich, Eduardo Nasi, and Nicole Witt, for their notes — my eternal gratitude. To Willian Vieira and Silvia Massimini Felix for their impeccable work.

To Anna Lee, for her support in this process and the lifetime lessons.

To Rafael Diel Schenkel, forest ranger and head of the Turvo State Park, for the interviews, classes, and field trips; also to Vilmar Grutzman, ranger; and Letícia Sell Reschke, park employee, for the research material.

To all of Turvo's rangers and employees.

To Antonio Carlos Venancio Aniceto, babalorixá and environmental manager, for the guidance and the protection.

In memoriam: Bruno Pereira and Dom Phillips.

Here ends Morgana Kretzmann's
The Red Earth.

The first edition of this book was printed
and bound at LSC Communications
in Harrisonburg, Virginia, July 2026.

A NOTE ON THE TYPE

This novel was set in Silva, a serif typeface created by Brazilian designer Daniel Sabino for Blackletra Type Foundry in 2015. Widely praised for both efficiency and readability, it features a well-balanced combination of slightly condensed proportions and robust serifs.

HARPERVIA

An imprint dedicated to publishing international voices,
offering readers a chance to encounter other lives and other
points of view via the language of the imagination.